M000234059

KISS ME, DUKE

League of Unweddable Gentlemen, Book 5

TAMARA
GILL

CHAPTER 1

Rome Italy, 1829

They had arrived. Finally. Molly stepped out of the carriage and stretched, basked in the warm Mediterranean sun that warmed her blood and healed the many aches and pains from weeks of travel. Rome. Just the thought of where she was sent a thrill down her spine and expectation thrumming through her blood.

So many wonderful places to visit and see, and thanks to her wonderful friends back in London, and the Duke of Whitstone, month-long lodgings at the Villa Maius had been secured for her. The gentleman who resided here was from home, but his servants would care for her and her companion for the short time they would be in the city.

The front door to the villa opened, and a gray-haired, voluptuous woman came out onto the street, her smile as warm as the sun shining down on her back.

"*Signora*, Molly Clare, welcome. Welcome to Rome. Come, we shall serve refreshments for you. You must be exhausted."

Molly smiled, relieved to be welcomed so lovingly at the home. She did not know anything of Mr. Farley, who lived here, other than he was friends with the Duke of Whitstone. There had always been a little niggling concern within her that the staff may be annoyed at her arrival, being unknown to them as she was, but it would not seem to be so.

"Thank you for having me. I hope it is not too much trouble that I'm here." She walked in off the street into a small foyer that led onto a large, rectangular room partly roofed. A fountain sat in its center, a naked cherub squirting water from his mouth. Looking up, Molly noted the opening in the roof sat directly over the fountain, and in ancient times, it would be the place the villa would have collected its water for the family.

"Oh, no no no. We're very happy to have you here." The servant ordered a tall, dark-haired man to attend to the luggage while she walked them toward a set of stairs. "Mr. Armstrong is not here. He is away in Naples for the duration of your stay, and we have been expecting you. He informed us all before he left last month to care for you well. You have mutual friends, yes?"

Molly looked about the villa. Mosaic-tiled floors adorned the space, images of Roman life, of agricultural scenes and animals. All lower-floor rooms had their windows open, the curtains billowing with the warm, Mediterranean air. The breeze smelled of salt and spices, of oranges and freshly cut grass. She stopped a moment, taking in the view from one of the windows she could see through a doorway. The courtyard garden, full of olive trees, beckoned her to sit and savor its beauty.

"We do, yes. The Duke of Whitstone. Although I have

never met Mr. Armstrong, I am very grateful to him for allowing me to stay here."

The housekeeper beamed, seemingly well pleased at her compliment of her employer. "He is the best of men whom I'm sorry you shall not have the honor of meeting." The woman started up the stone stairs. "I'm Maria, my dear, the housekeeper of Villa Maius. Should you need anything at all, merely let me know, and I shall do all that I can to make your stay enjoyable."

"Thank you." They climbed the stairs, the second floor opened up to a large, rectangular room with reclining wicker chairs. A balcony stood at the end of the room. Molly could not pass without taking in the view. She stepped out onto the balcony, the breath catching in her lungs. The view overlooked the street they had entered on. At this height, it gave her a better vantage point of the city beyond. Rome. Its glory spread out before her like a gift from the gods. Her fingers curled around the stone balustrade, anchoring herself so she would not run from the villa and see firsthand the ancient city. Sounds wafted up to tease her and urge her to leave and explore.

Soon, she promised. As soon as she had bathed and had a restoring cup of tea.

"The center of Rome is only a short walk from here. At the other end of the villa is another room similar to this that overlooks the river Tiber. I can always have the carriage put at your disposal, however, if you do not want to walk. To see the Vatican, you shall have to avail yourself of the vehicle."

Excitement thrummed through her veins, and she leaned out over the railing, spying a few people out on the streets, some taking in the sights while others plied their trade. "What a magnificent city. I have always wanted to tour, and now I can. I cannot believe it."

"I am dreading the return journey, however," her companion, Miss Sinclair said, joining her and staring down at the city with a disgruntled air. "Shall we have tea?"

Molly was reluctant to leave the magnificent view, one she longed to be part of, and nor would she allow Miss Sinclair's dislike of the distances they had traversed to dampen her excitement. If her companion did not wish to see Rome, she could stay here at the villa. Molly went about London most of the time on her own, it would not be out of character for her.

"Yes, let's, and then I can get started on exploring this wonderful city."

"Would you like to have tea on the balcony, *Signora* Molly?"

"Thank you, yes," she replied, seeing the outdoor setting and sitting. Servants bustled about the home, bringing up their trunks to the rooms. Molly could almost pinch herself just to confirm that she was indeed here in Rome. Her time was precious, only a month, and then they would be on the return journey back to England. Travel would take several weeks, and she wanted to visit some other cities on the continent before returning to London and the new Season.

The tea was sweet and refreshing, and lovingly the housekeeper had made some biscuits with almonds through them, which squelched her rumbling stomach.

Molly leaned back in her chair, placing down her napkin, well-sated after the fleeting repast. "Shall we finish the tour of the house, see our rooms and then decide where to go first?"

"Of course, Miss Molly," Miss Sinclair said, yawning.

It had been a long day, but Molly was too excited, had waited too long to be in Rome to lie down for the afternoon. She wanted to explore, walk the streets, visit the markets, and be part of the culture here in this ancient city.

"If you're tired, Miss Sinclair, I can always go out without you. I do not mind."

Miss Sinclair's lips pursed into a disapproving, thin line. "No, that would never do. You need to have a chaperone and company to keep you safe. I will simply have to endure it."

"I do not wish for you to endure Rome. I want you to enjoy it as much as I intend on doing."

"I do not believe that will be possible, Miss Molly. I have an aversion to heat, and if it did not escape your notice, it is very hot outside."

Molly turned toward the balcony, the slight breeze wafting in through the doors cooled her skin. Yes it was warm, but England was always so very cold. How could anyone not make use of such beautiful weather and explore it?

The housekeeper stepped forward, catching Molly's eye. "We have a manservant here, Miss Clare. He would be more than happy to escort you about Rome so you may see some of our wonderful city."

Molly smiled at Miss Sinclair. "See, I shall be perfectly safe. You may have this afternoon to rest and recuperate, and we shall come together for dinner this evening before tonight's ball."

"You intend to attend Lord and Lady Dalton's ball this evening? Even though we only arrived today?"

"Of course I intend to go." Molly shook her head at

her companion, having gained the sense that she did not want to go or do anything while they were here. The prospect was not helpful, nor would it be possible. Molly had four weeks to visit this wonderful city, and she would simply have to ignore her companion's complaints about seeing everything they could in that time.

"Maria, will you show me to my room, please?"

The housekeeper bustled down a wide passageway until she came to a room that overlooked more of the villa grounds, lawns, and gardens that swam with a variety of colors. The tinkling sound of water carried up to her, and she looked for the fountain but could not see it from her room. She would have to go downstairs to find it herself.

Her room was a tiled mosaic floor that was made out in a variety of blossoming flowers. Her bed was large, opulent with its coverlet and abundance of pillows. She, too, was partial to lots of pillows on beds. It somehow made them look complete. Perfect.

A small writing desk occupied the space before one window, and a large settee sat before her fire. Although she did not believe she would need that at all while she was here in Rome. Not with it being so warm.

"There is freshwater and linens behind the screen for you, Miss Molly. When you're ready to go out, come downstairs, and I shall fetch Marcus for you. He will keep you safe and show you all the best sites Rome has on offer."

"Thank you so much. I cannot tell you how thrilled I am about being here."

The housekeeper smiled before leaving her to her ablutions, the sound of Miss Sinclair's voice as she was taken to her room echoing down the hall.

Molly walked to the small balcony her room had and

glanced down at the garden. She raised her face to the sun, breathing deep. What an idyllic location to live. One could get used to such a place and never return home to rainy, dreary old London.

CHAPTER 2

*H*e wasn't supposed to be in Rome. He'd promised his close friend the Duke of Whitstone that he would leave Miss Molly Clare alone for the month she was visiting the ancient city. But he could not. Not because he wished to meet the chit—he'd long thrown away any notion of making a grand match or even trying to court a lady.

Business brought him back to Rome a month earlier than planned. A letter from his brother's steward in London never bode well. What had his brother done now that was so very bad that the black sheep of the family had to be notified?

Lord Hugh Farley, younger brother to the Duke of St. Albans, pushed through the small door off the street that led into his Roman villa and strode through the gardens, headed for his office. He waved to a couple of his staff who were picking vegetables, ignoring the fact they looked a little shocked at his return. His housekeeper Maria doubly so when he strode into the atrium.

"I shall have lunch brought into my office, please,

Maria." He half-laughed at the woman's expression. "Do not look so shocked at my being here. I do live here as you well know."

The housekeeper made an awkward chuckle before following close on his heels. "You have Miss Molly Clare here, *Signore* Hugh. Do you not remember she is to stay a month?"

"I have not forgot, but I received a letter from my brother's steward that I must attend to." His man of business in Rome had sent word to him, telling him to return from Naples as soon as possible. It was unfortunate that Miss Clare was here at the same time as he, but this was his home, and she had a companion, it would not be too scandalous, surely.

"I do not intend to ruin her, Maria. Do amend your distress."

Another awkward laugh from his housekeeper rent loudly in the room. Hugh glanced up at her, not missing that she was now wringing her hands in her apron. "You disapprove."

"She's unmarried, *Signore*. You, too, remain unmarried. We could weather any storm of her being here when you were not at home, but now that you are, tongues will wag. Whether those tongues are in Rome or London."

"Let them wag. I have business to attend to, and she has a companion. There is little we can do about it. I shall not allow society to rule my life." God knows he'd allowed enough of that in London along with his family. The thought of his brother, his mother, soured the taste in his mouth. He picked up his penknife and sliced open the missive.

"Lunch, Maria. If you please."

As if remembering herself, she bobbed a quick curtsy

and left the room. Hugh opened the parchment and read. His blood ran cold at the black, cursive words that lay out before his eyes.

His Grace, the Duke of St. Albans, had passed away after a carriage accident. We here inform Lord Hugh Farley that you are now the Duke of St. Albans, heir to St. Albans Abbey in Kent, Brentwood House in Surrey, and Clare Castle in Ireland.

The rest of the missive blurred at the thought of his brother no longer living. This letter was already a month old. Hugh leaned back in his chair, staring blankly at the wall before him.

It could not be.

Henry was dead? His only brother. Another letter sat on his desk, the neat, flowing script that of his younger sister, Sarah. He tore it open, not bothering with the penknife. She was less diplomatic, having never been very good at making her words less blunt and to the point. Her letter contained details about their brother's demise, of his foolhardy bet with the gentleman who formed his London set. They had planned to race a curricle from London to Southampton, and Henry had overturned the vehicle, killing himself instantly. She implored him to return to London post-haste and take up the position as the Duke of St. Albans.

Hugh scrunched up the letter, throwing it onto his desk. London could go hang. The fickle *ton* may very well forgive him the scandal that dogged his every move in that city, but he would never forgive London.

The bastards.

The amused, excited voice of a woman flittered downstairs before the boots on his staircase echoed in the foyer. From where Hugh sat, he could see who came and went in the atrium outside his tablinum. In the past ten years that he'd lived in Rome, he realized that there had never been a woman under this roof, save the servants of course.

He watched the threshold of his door, wanting to see what this Miss Molly Clare looked like. His friend, The Duke of Whitstone, one of only a few he had left in the world, had written to him asking for assistance in housing Miss Clare. He could not refuse.

Every year, Hugh traveled to Naples to his vineyard there, so there were no problems offering his Roman villa while he moved to his estate in the country.

A woman in an azure-colored dress stepped into his line of sight, and the breath in his lungs seized. She wasn't a young woman as he thought she may be, but a woman, her figure filling out her day gown in the most promising way.

Her hair was inky black and tied up into a motif of loose curls, some of which had already fallen out and bounced about her slender shoulders. A bonnet hung from her wrist from a vivid-blue ribbon, and a pelisse lay over her arm. Everything about her embodied what he had left behind in London. Had he stayed in England, he could now be married to a woman as appealing as Miss Clare. Had a family, children playing about his hessian boots. A pang of nostalgia thrummed through him over everything that he had lost by leaving London to live in Rome.

By following the rules and doing what he was told.

Not that it was his fault that he had to come away, his brother Henry had ordered him to take the fall for his wayward actions. Hugh had refused of course, until both his mother and brother had told him his ruin was done. That the *ton* would not accept him from that moment onward. His choice was clear, leave England or face being cut off socially and financially.

A younger son of a duke, he had money, of course, but not enough that would keep him for long. He had not studied law or the church as one might to live. A stupid mistake.

With nowhere else to turn, he had made some demands of his own. His brother would fund his living here in Rome. Purchase him a villa and house in Naples, a locale he had enjoyed when on the grand tour only two years before. A small price for his brother to pay since Hugh was the one losing everything, and his family.

Miss Clare slipped on her bonnet, laughing at something Marcus, his manservant, said to her before they both walked from the atrium. "Maria," Hugh called, catching his housekeeper's eye.

Maria bustled into his office, a small smile playing about her mouth. "*Signore?* You called."

"Where is Marcus taking Miss Clare?" He placed the letters from his brother's steward and Sarah into his drawer, locking it away.

"She wished to visit Trevi Fountain. I think they will then walk to the food market, Piazza Navona after that."

"I shall dine with her tonight, explain the reasons why I'm back in Rome. I'm sure she'll understand that business has brought me home." It'll also allow him the opportunity to ask her about London and what the latest *on dit* was. He'd not dined with a woman in an age. In fact, he could not remember the last time he'd slept with one either. Too long, not that he was looking to Miss Clare to scratch that particular itch, but even so, she was attractive with her womanly curves, pretty eyes, and warm laugh. Dinner this evening may be an enjoyable affair and a good distraction after the news he'd just received.

"Of course, *Signore*. I shall get your luncheon right away."

"Thank you, Maria."

Hugh slid a piece of parchment before him, picking up a quill and dipping it into the black ink. He started a reply to his brother's steward. He wished he could feel an ounce of despair, sorrow even, at the death of his brother. He did not. He would write to Sarah, and console her as best he could. Even with the thousands of miles that separated them, she had never turned against him at least, had believed his side of the story, especially since she knew all too well what a reprobate Henry was. Even so, she would be hurting right now, she had loved them both being her only brothers, her only family left, no matter how wild or vexing Henry could be at times.

Hugh wished he could be sorry, but his brother having joined in with the *ton* allowed the lies to percolate through society until his name was mud, and not admitting to his wrongdoing in the whole sorry mess was something Hugh could not forgive.

And now he was the Duke of St. Albans. A title and responsibility he'd never wanted.

Damn it all to blasted hell.

～

*M*olly returned to the villa late in the afternoon after a day of walking the streets of Rome. The Spanish Steps, the markets, and the beautiful, awe-inspiring Trevi Fountain. Marcus had allowed her to visit whatever seized her attention while keeping her safe. It had been the perfect first day in Rome, and she could not wait until another commenced tomorrow.

13

She entered the villa, the cooler air inside the atrium a welcome reprieve after a day in the sun. Molly slipped off her bonnet, perspiration moistening her hair and sticking to her neck. She would need to bathe before dinner. Her stomach rumbled at the thought of food as she stepped on the first stair heading upstairs.

"Miss Clare, how very good to meet you."

The deep, gravelly baritone startled her, and she gasped, turning to see where the voice had come from. She felt her mouth pop open at the sight of the man before her. His tall, athletic frame was enough to turn any woman's eye, but his face was beyond stunning. His cheekbones seemed chiseled from marble, similar to the statues she'd seen this afternoon. His raven colored hair was longer than it ought to be, was tied back off his face, and the shadowing of an unshaven jawline made her mouth dry. Her whole body shivered at his presence, and she swallowed, hoping her voice would still work.

Molly stepped off the stair and walked toward him, giving her a moment to compose herself. She met his clear, smoky-black orbs, and something inside her thrummed, came alive at his proximity.

She jerkily held out her hand for him to take. "Sir, I do not believe we've been introduced." His mouth lifted into a delicious grin, and she bit her lip, unsure what to do with herself when he smiled. Heat crept over her face at her wayward thoughts. His eyes roamed over her features, and she schooled her emotions, willing her racing heart to calm.

"I'm Mr. Armstrong. I live here. The Duke of Whitstone, I believe, is a mutual friend of ours." He picked up her hand, kissing her gloveless fingers. The feel of his lips on her skin sent a bolt of awareness up her arm, and she stepped back, placing well-needed space between them.

"Oh yes, Mr. Armstrong. How do you do? Thank you so much for offering me your home during my stay here. I hope you did not mind that his grace asked on my behalf for accommodations."

"Not at all." He gestured toward the stairs. "I shall return you to your room. I'm sure you wish to freshen up before dinner."

"I would yes," she said, starting up the stairs and hoping he hadn't noticed her disarray too much. "Have you known the duke for long?" Molly hadn't queried too much how the duke and Mr. Armstrong were known to each other, even though she was so very grateful they were. She had not wanted to stay in a hotel here in the city. She'd wanted to visit Rome and stay in an ancient villa if she could. Being here would probably be the only time she would visit the city in her life, and she had wanted to make it memorable.

"We were in school together at Eton and socialized in the same social sphere." He walked beside her, his hands clasped behind his back. She surreptitiously took in his attire and liked what she saw. He seemed to have the air of a titled gentleman, but that wasn't the case from what she did know.

His tan breeches and highly polished buckskin boots went well with his casual attire—no superfine coat or waistcoat for this Mr. Armstrong. A simple shirt and loosely tied cravat were all that he needed. It suited him, and she liked the casual way of life here in the city.

"Whitstone stayed here when he traveled abroad a few years ago."

She nodded, listening to him talk of their friendship,

savoring the sound of his voice, like rich, delicious chocolate that melted on one's tongue. Molly cleared her throat, not sure why she imagined Mr. Armstrong in such a way. "Are you staying in Rome for some time, or are you just traveling through? I understood that you were going to be away from home for several weeks."

"I was going to be away, but I had an urgent letter from London that brought me back. I hope you will continue to stay here, Miss Clare, even with me ensconced under the same roof. You have a chaperone, I understand."

The thought of having Mr. Armstrong under the roof sent a thrill down her spine, and for a moment, she regretted her decision to bring a chaperone with her to Rome. Molly was, after all, a woman well beyond her first blush. It would be unnatural for her to look upon such a handsome specimen of a man and not imagine all sorts of naughty things with him. She'd read enough books on anatomy and the art of lovemaking to know that she would not be adverse to a man such as the one who towered beside her, taking her to his bed. His strong, athletic build, well-defined arms, and large hands displayed a healthy, active gentleman well in his prime.

"I do have a chaperone. Miss Sinclair is her name. I'm sure with her being here with me, nothing untoward can be said about you being back in Rome." Molly let out a self-deprecating laugh. "Not that anyone cares what I do in any case, save my friends."

"Why is that?" he asked, frowning and halting his progress at the top of the stairs. "Why would no one care what you do? I cannot believe such a statement."

Molly stopped and glanced up at Mr. Armstrong, losing herself in his comforting stare. "While I may have friends who are well placed in society, I am not one of them. My family was good enough to help me achieve my dream of traveling to Rome, but there will not be another such venture. I'm not certain what I shall do when I return to England."

"You do not wish to marry?" Mr. Armstrong ran a hand through his hair, cringing. "Apologies, Miss Clare. I should not ask you such personal questions. It is not my place."

She smiled, reaching out and clasping his arm. The moment her hand touched the bare flesh, she knew it for the mistake it was. To feel his warmth, the sprinkling of coarse hair beneath her fingers shot longing through her body. Only made her want to touch more of him.

"I do not mind. If you're to be here with me and we're to spend more time together, you will learn soon enough that I am who I am and have no issues with being truthful. I cannot stand it when women dissemble, say things that one has to try to puzzle out. I think some women of my acquaintance think such a thing is amusing, whereas to me, it's merely annoying."

Mr. Armstrong barked out a laugh, taking her hand and placing it on his arm as they started back toward her room. "I think, Miss Clare, that you and I shall get along well. I, too, am opposed to disassembling and falsehoods. It is why I live in Rome. I could not live in London with the despicable gossipmongers who live to ruin other people's lives."

Molly stared down at the mosaic-tiled floor. His words held a hardened edge to them as if he were cut by the *ton* itself and knew firsthand what could happen to an unsuspecting or vague fellow in the *ton*.

"I hope your letter from home was not bad news, Mr. Armstrong. I should hate to be an inconvenience," she said, hoping to change the subject away from London, and the pitfalls one could sink into without too much trouble.

He stopped at her bedroom door, and the scent of wisteria floated through the air. "You are not an inconvenience, not at all. I'm glad that you're here and I intend to show you about Rome myself. It has been too long since I took the time to enjoy the city, the people. I will have no argument on the point, either. You're my guest to spoil, and spoil you I shall."

Molly stood before him, taken aback by his kindness. His sweetness toward a woman that he did not know. Perhaps his time in Rome had been lonely, and having her here allowed him to present his grand city to her. To spend time with a woman from his homeland who shared mutual friends.

"You're too kind." Molly opened her bedroom door, turning to face him. "I do not know how to thank you for having me here and being my escort. I shall tell Whitstone of your kindness. You can be certain of that."

Mr. Armstrong nodded, stepping back and placing space between them. His eyes met hers and held. Molly's heart sped up once more.

"No need for that. Your company will be thanks enough."

Warmth touched her cheeks, and Molly prayed he thought her flush was from her tour of Rome and not his sweet words or company. Which, of course, was exactly why it was.

CHAPTER 3

The following morning, Hugh sat at his breakfast table that overlooked the gardens and read his mail that Marcus had brought in to him. Another letter from Sarah told him of Henry's funeral and the outpouring of grief that the *ton* had managed to feign. He doubted anyone in society was honest and capable of any emotions other than greed and hate.

The sound of slippered feet caught his attention, and he looked up just as Miss Clare stepped up into the room, a small, welcoming smile on her pretty mouth.

"Mr. Armstrong. Good morning. What a beautiful day it looks to be." She sat to his side, looking over the abundance of food to choose from that sat before her.

He had taken to serving himself since living in Rome, and having the food on the table instead of a sideboard was much easier for both him and his servants.

"It is going to be lovely, and because that is so, I have an idea."

She glanced at him just as she placed a piece of bacon on her plate. "Even better. What is this idea?"

Her exuberance for life, for seeing the city he now called home, sent a kick through his blood. For years he had gone about with the same routine, rarely venturing out to socialize, keeping to himself and running his vineyard. To show off his home, his city to someone who did not know who he was, was liberating.

Made him feel like the young gentleman he once was in England that had his whole life ahead of him and little to worry about.

"You'll need your best walking boots, for I'm going to take you to visit the Colosseum. We'll return here in the early afternoon before it gets too hot." He wanted to take her to the Colosseum, show her the majestic building, and, if permitted, take her into the building's underground apartments where the gladiators waited to live or die.

Miss Clare's smile lit up the room, and he found himself grinning back at her. "Are you certain I'm not taking up too much of your time? I do not want to drag you away from your work."

He waved her concerns away, pouring her a cup of tea before finishing his own. "Not at all. I want to do this. Whitstone would never forgive me if I did not take care of you and show you about." Not that he needed the excuse of his friend to make him escort her around. Miss Clare was a sensible, intelligent woman. It was no chore being in her presence.

The walk to the historical site took only half an hour, the stroll through the winding cobbled and paved streets pleasant on a warm morning. Behind them, Marcus and Miss Clare's chaperone, Miss Sinclair, chatted and seemed to be getting along quite well.

The Colosseum had several arched doors to enter by, and Hugh pulled Molly through the first one they came across, walking into a large, curving tunnel, several degrees cooler than the air outside.

"What an amazing building this is." Miss Clare stood looking out over the Colosseum, her mouth agape at the sight that beheld her. It was a common reaction and one that Hugh himself had had when he first visited the place.

They climbed stairs heading up to the tiered seat section that overlooked the central orchestra and stage. "This was all once marble-veneered, but over the years, people have stripped it of its precious decorations, and the weather has not helped. What a sight it must have made. Can you just imagine?" he asked, watching her. Warmth seeped into his bones at the unguarded pleasure that blossomed on her face. She took every ounce, every nuance of the building, no doubt imagining it in its prime.

"To think gladiators fought and died in the arena below us. And you said we might be able to go beneath?"

"Of course. It is no problem." They walked along what was left of the seating areas that surveyed the central stage —the overwhelming magnitude of the place something he'd never forget. "I haven't been here for some years. I'm glad that I'm here with you today, Miss Clare. To reacquaint myself with the city that I now call home." And he was. She was a breath of fresh air into his life that had stagnated of late. He had his investments, his villa at Naples, and the vineyard, but no social life. Not when it came to attending balls and parties thrown by visitors from London to Rome. People who knew him and what he'd been accused of.

"To imagine the roars of the people barracking for their favorite gladiator echoes still through this old stone. I adore history if you have not noticed already. It was one of the reasons why I wanted to come here."

"What was the other reason?" he asked, enjoying himself more than he ought, especially for a man who had been notified of his brother's death only the day before. Not that Henry ever cared about anyone other than himself. Even so, as a brother, one ought to feel something. Regret, sadness. He felt numb. He'd lost all respect and affection for his sibling when he'd turned his back on him in London and let him face alone the savage wolves that were the *ton*.

"My friends." She smiled at him over her shoulder before leaning on the stone railing and studied what was left of the combat ring. "I love them, do not mistake me, but they're determined to see me wed. Married off and happily situated just as they all are."

"You do not wish to be married?" Today it would seem he was full of inappropriateness. He was talking to an unmarried maid of her love affairs. That was not to be borne. Even so, he was curious why someone would run thousands of miles away to evade marriage.

"If I fall in love and marry, that is all very well, but if I do not, that is all very well. I'm not a young woman, Mr. Armstrong. If you have not guessed already."

"You are not old either, Miss Clare. There would be many a gentleman who would offer for you, I would think."

She chuckled, shaking her head. The action caused a curl to fall loose from her motif and bounce upon her shoulder. His gaze dipped to the unblemished skin where the coil sat, a fine collarbone pulling the eye toward her sweet neck and ample bosom that her walking gown failed to conceal. Miss Clare was extremely appealing. The word lush floated through his mind, and he severed his inspection of her before she noticed.

"You would be wrong, Mr. Armstrong. I have not had one offer in all the years I have graced the London ballrooms. But I am happy for my friends, each of their husbands I adore and love like a brother. I shall never be lonely, do not fear, but I have come to accept that perhaps my time has passed, and so before my life does too, I must seize the day and see this wonderful world for myself."

"I admire your will, Miss Clare. I wish more women had such a strong constitution. My sister certainly does. You would like her, I think."

"You have a sister? Who is she? Maybe I have met her before?"

Hugh pointed to the stairs that led down into the bowels of the Colosseum, taking Miss Clare's hand and pulling her toward the entrance. "Sarah is her name, but she is some years younger than me and for years has refused to attend the Season. She spends most of her time in the country with her horses and dogs."

"I think then perhaps I shall like her very much."

He chuckled. The morning drifted by pleasantly. They took an hour-long tour of the underground of the Colosseum. It was an agreeable day and Hugh found himself laughing a lot more than he had in years. They returned to the villa, dusty and weary after their excursion, just as the sun reached the hottest time of the day.

Hugh pulled Miss Clare to a stop in the atrium, not willing to relinquish her hand. "Will you dine with me on the terrace this evening? I feel I do not wish for this day to end."

A light blush stole over her features, and the urge to reach out, touch her pretty face, was overwhelming. He had not thought to meet his house guest, nevertheless find her so sweet and charming. When the Duke of Whitstone had suggested that he help him in housing Miss Clare, he'd imagined a young, spoiled debutante. One who would simper and preen as they all did and drive his servants to distraction. He'd fled to Naples imagining such a visitor. How very opportune and fortunate he was that Miss Clare was nothing of the kind.

He liked her.

"That would be delightful, thank you, Mr. Armstrong. I shall rest for the afternoon and see you at dinner."

He bowed, watching as she went up the stairs, admiring the sway of her hips in her pretty dress. He turned, rubbing a hand over his jaw and striding to his tablinum in need of a stiff drink. He'd offered protection for her for the few weeks she was in Rome. He wasn't to molest her. Whitstone would beat him to a pulp should he seduce the chit, even so, sometimes, a good beating was worth it if the woman who warmed your bed was as delectable as Miss Clare certainly was.

With such thoughts, was it any wonder he was banished from England.

~

*D*inner that evening was everything Molly missed from England. Mr. Armstrong's cook had outdone herself with a roast lamb, vegetables, and turtle soup. Dessert consisted of seasonal fruits along with jelly and cakes. Even so, no matter how delicious the fare, it did not make her one ounce homesick. She loved being here in Rome, visiting the ancient city and meeting its people.

She glanced at Mr. Armstrong, so very imposing, intelligent, and too good-looking to be unattached. Not that she knew much about his past, only that he was the Duke of

Whitstone's friend, and therefore someone she could trust. There was probably a gaggle of women waiting about Rome for him to call. For all that she knew, he may have a mistress who was missing him.

Molly shifted on her seat, taking a fortifying sip of her wine. She didn't want to think of him with anyone else. The idea of Mr. Armstrong in a passionate embrace with another woman made her want to cast up her accounts. An absurd reaction since she'd only known him a day.

But there was something about him she liked. He was kind and attentive and did not mock her many questions regarding life here or the treasures the city held. Their day at the Colosseum had been marvelous, and he'd been patient with her as she had taken it all in, no matter how long that took her.

Not all men would be so thoughtful.

"Shall we adjourn to the tablinum? I have two chairs that sit before a fire in that room. I know it is warm during the day, but I still like a little heat at night. I suppose you may take the Englishman out of England, but you cannot take England out of an Englishman."

"That would be lovely, yes."

Mr. Armstrong stood and came and helped her with her chair. "Bring your wine. We shall have after-dinner drinks together."

She did as he bade, before he reached out, placing her hand on his arm to escort her from the room. The moment her fingers touched his shirtsleeve, heat threaded up her arm and settled in her stomach. She swallowed, schooling her features, not wanting him to see just how much he discombobulated her. He would think her a fool for reacting so, especially when they hardly knew each other.

"You're very brave," he said, guiding her toward a part

of the house she had not seen as yet. "Not many women would venture abroad with a companion and not much else. Whatever possessed you?"

"Do you reproach me for such a journey, Mr. Armstrong?" she asked, sitting in one of the leatherback chairs before the hearth. Mr. Armstrong walked over to a decanter and poured himself a whiskey.

"Not at all, but I am interested. Women do travel, of course, but they're either widowed or traveling with their husbands. I'm curious, that is all."

Molly thought back on her cousin Laura, how she had suffered through the birth of her son and subsequently paid for that birth with her life. The child only hours later following his mama to the grave.

"Many years ago, I was told never to wait for what I wanted. That if we laid all our hopes on those of others, we were destined for sadness. I promised myself I would not settle for anything other than love if I married, and if that did not eventuate that I would resolve myself to be fulfilled with only me for company. That I would not miss out on the world's gifts merely because I was unable to be someone's wife."

Mr. Armstrong took a sip of his amber liquid, watching her over the brim of his glass. "Your friend sounds a little jaded."

"She was and rightfully so. Although, I promised her that I would never be taken in by false promises and sweet words, and I haven't so far. Now at my age," Molly said, smiling a little. "It is becoming less likely each year."

Mr. Armstrong cocked one brow. Her stomach twisted at the wicked, amused glance he threw her. "From where I am sitting, Miss Clare, you are far from invulnerable." He finished his drink, setting it down with a clink. "Would you like to attend a party with me this evening? They are acquaintances, business associates I deal with in Rome. They're not titled or whom you're used to socializing with back in London, but they are good company and would welcome you if you attended."

Heat crept across her skin, and Molly took a sip of her wine, hoping her flush would not spread across her cheeks. She was not invulnerable? Whatever did he mean by such a statement? "I shall be safe enough. I have you to guard me. Have I not?" she said.

He chuckled, nodding. "Of course."

"Then I shall like to attend with you. If you're certain, it will be welcome." She studied him a moment, wondering about his past also. "You left London yourself. Why is it that you ended up in Rome?"

He frowned, sitting forward, his attention lost on the burning wood in the grate. "I disagreed with my family and could not stay. They granted funds to start my life here in Rome, and I accepted. I shall never return to London."

The thought that she would never see this man grace the floorboards of the great London homes left a pang of regret to lodge in her stomach. She didn't want to never see him again, and it was unlikely that she would ever return to Rome.

"I'm sorry to hear that, Mr. Armstrong. I'm not certain that I could be estranged from my family forever."

"Sometimes," he said, "estrangement is necessary for one's sanity. In any case, I have lived here for many years and love it as much as I loved my life before leaving London. I no longer miss it too much."

"May I ask one more question?" she asked, finishing her drink and placing it, too, on the table before them both. His gaze met hers, and she fought the urge to fan her face. He was so very intense. His attention fixed on hers with such fervor that one couldn't help but think he was reading her mind. No gentleman had ever paid so much attention to her or spent so much time.

"If you wish to?" He leaned back in his chair, waiting.

"What is your given name?" she asked.

All tension fled his features, and he chuckled, his smile just as devastating as the sound of his deep, rich voice that was suggestive as hell.

"Hugh. My name is Hugh, Miss Clare. And yours?" he queried.

"Molly," she said, feeling oddly embarrassed by their admissions. "May I ask one more question?" she continued, daring herself to be bold. To seek what she wanted. Not that asking for a man's name was so very scandalous, but women were taught not to be so forward. A lesson hard to unlearn.

"Yes," he said.

"May I call you Hugh instead of Mr. Armstrong when we're alone, such as we are now? Or when we're looking about Rome?"

"So I'm to accompany you about Rome more than once?"

"Well, I ah…" Molly wasn't certain what to say. There was no guarantee that Mr. Armstrong was even staying in Rome during her stay here. He may only be here a day and then traveling back to Naples.

He stood, coming over to her and pulling her from her seat. His hand was large and strong, his fingers entwining with hers. Heat licked at her core, her body unlike its steadfast, no-nonsense self it always was. He made her want things she'd never wanted before. He made her want him. She looked up at Hugh, unable to step back and give them the necessary space to be proper.

"It would be a pleasure to be here in Rome for the duration of your stay, to be your tour guide, and yes, you may call me Hugh, but only on one condition."

"Condition?" She cleared her throat. Why did she sound so breathless? He would imagine her fascination with him in no time if she did not get a hold of her emotions. She was being a silly chit, and would start to sound like an adoring debutante soon if she did not guard her heart. She was not in Rome to lose her head to a man. She was here to tour the city. He was merely a polite host. A gentleman determined to make her stay here a happy one. A memory that would last a lifetime once she returned to England. "What condition is that?"

He lifted her hand to his lips, kissing her fingers. His lips were soft. So very smooth and warm, and her mind imagined where else those lips would feel so sweet. She bit her lip, fighting to stem her wayward thoughts.

"That I may call you Molly in turn."

She nodded, unable to form words right at that moment. If she were as bold as her friend Evie or Willow, she would close the space between them and take what she wanted. A kiss. Her first kiss. But she could not. She had never been bold, not in that way, at least. "I would like that," she said at length, taking a welcome breath as he nodded once and started for the door.

"We leave in an hour for the party. Are you able to be ready by then?" he asked, stopping at the threshold of the room.

"Of course," Molly said, watching him go and taking a moment to compose herself. Heavens forbid, she had almost swooned at his attention. What an intoxicating man he was, and a little mysterious. She had not heard of the Armstrong's in London, and it was interesting that he went to school with Whitstone and was of that social sphere and yet not titled. A mystery, and one she would untangle if she were able while she was here.

But tonight was reserved for dancing and fun. Experience what society was hundreds of miles away from the one she graced in England. And if she were lucky enough, perhaps Mr. Armstrong, Hugh as she would forever think of him, would offer his hand for a dance. A waltz in his arms sounded quite the perfect end to a most assuredly ideal day.

CHAPTER 4

$\mathscr{T}$he party was an opulent affair. The society in Rome was varied, and he was glad the social sphere he graced now knew nothing of his true identity or the family in which he came from.

Even so, their host's villa that sat overlooking Rome was grander and larger than his own. The family had made their wealth in wine and had houses all over Italy.

Tonight the atrium was the location of the entertainment, to the side in the tablinum sat an orchestra that played both modern and ancient tunes. Similar to his home, the atrium here was tiled in mosaic flooring, a central pond the main feature. This villa, however, being on a larger scale, the opening in the atrium was large enough that one could look up to the heavens and see the night sky in its full glory. Millions of stars framed just for them.

Servants carried around platters of drinks and supper, no need to stop the festivities to sit and eat like back in London. Hugh stood beside a Grecian statue, sipping his wine as he watched Molly speak with their hostess. Her laughter carried to where he stood, and he could tell that she was enjoying their conversation.

She was a beautiful woman, and the more time he spent with her, the more he looked forward to the next time they met. While getting dressed for this evening's reception, he'd thought of what they could do tomorrow, where to take her and what to see. He hoped that she would like his choice and continue to allow him to be her escort while in Rome.

For a moment, he allowed himself to imagine that he'd never left London, that he'd been able to meet Molly in society and court her as he liked. She certainly brought a calmness wherever she went, and he found himself wishing they had met before the scandal that sent him abroad broke.

His mother and brother conspiring for him to take the fall for his brother's indiscretion ensured he was no longer part of that family. It goaded his pride that he'd had to live on the funds his brother sent to ensure his survival for some years, but for the past eight, he'd not had to. Out of spite, perhaps, he still cashed those checks from London, but turned around and donated the funds to the women of Rome, who found themselves *enceinte* and without a protector or husband.

It was the least he could do to try to honor Laura in some way, make recompense to the woman his brother had ruined.

"Why are you not dancing, Mr. Armstrong? You look well enough that I do believe you will survive a turn about the dancefloor."

He chuckled, reveling in her bright eyes and smiling mouth that he had an overwhelming urge to lean down toward and kiss. To test his theory that her lips were as soft and willing as he suspected. Or at least hoped.

"We're back to Mr. Armstrong? I did hope you would call me by my given name as we agreed."

She shrugged, taking a glass of champagne from a passing servant before taking a sip. "We're not alone, which was part of the agreement. What if someone should hear?"

"No one shall hear with all the noise of this party." He wanted to hear his name on her lips. For all his fleeing of England had left a sour taste in his mouth, having Molly here, an English woman who was sweet and kind, to hear his name spoken by her did odd things to his soul. Warmed it after ten years of being chilled.

"Very well," she said, smiling at him, the loveliest blush speckling her cheeks. "I shall do as you ask, but should anyone step nearby or other guests join us, we must revert to our formal names."

"Agreed," he said, turning back to take in the guests lest someone spy his marked attention on the woman who was lodging under his roof. He ought to leave, go to a hotel and stay there for the duration of her stay, but he could not, and for reasons he'd not think too far upon at present. "You have not danced as much as I thought you would."

"Oh, I've danced plenty, and you very well know it. Why I just finished a dance with Lord Brandon, whom I know from London. Do you know him?"

Hugh schooled his features as a knot of anxiety lodged in his gut. Was Lord Brandon in Rome? How did he not know? His attention slipped over the crowd, and it did not take him long to spy the earl, who was mutual friends with Duke Whitstone. A peer who was fully cognizant of why he'd fled his homeland.

"How do you know the earl?" he asked.

"Through the Duke and Duchess of Whitstone."

Hugh kept surreptitiously checking to see where Lord Brandon was situated. He was happy to see that within a few minutes of spying him, the gentleman and his handsome Italian wife were taking their leave of their hostess. He breathed deep, thankful his night had not ended with a confrontation between him and his lordship.

"Tell me how you came to know the Duchess of Whitstone? From the correspondence from His Grace? You're very close friends."

"We went to school with each other in France. Each of us was sent away from home for various reasons. I, because my parents feared that I would throw myself away on some rogue for reasons I shall not bore you with. Even so, we all met at Madame Dufour's Refining School for girls. Our friendship has never waned over the years, and although our lives do take us on different paths, we always are there for each other when needed."

Hugh wished he had such friends. He'd lost so many of his set when his brother had forced his scandal onto his shoulders. In hindsight, he should have made his brother clean up his own mess. Face the matrons of the *ton* looking down their noses at him for his ungentlemanly behavior. But they had not. Oh no, the future Duke Henry could not be besmirched by a woman of loose morals, even if that woman had been a childhood friend and neighbor.

"They sound like the best of people. You are lucky to have such friends."

She threw him a small smile, and the concern of him being outed to her for his brother's sin lessened. "I believe I am."

The strains of a waltz drifted across the warm night's

air, and Hugh placed down his glass of wine, bowing before Molly. "May I have this dance, Miss Clare?"

Without hesitation, she placed her silk-gloved fingers onto his palm, closing them tight about his hand. "I would like that very much, Mr. Armstrong."

Hugh led her out onto the dancefloor beside the central fountain. They took their places on the makeshift ballroom floor and waited for the music to begin.

His fingers closed about her waist, the tulle that sat over her emerald-green gown shimmered under the stars and hundreds of candles that the Costa family's servants had placed about the room. He pulled her close, not missing the moment her eyes flared at his action. As close as they now stood, it was not as close as he would like.

The gown was soft under his touch, her waist small and delicate. The music started, and he whirled her into the steps, spinning them before waltzing about the room. The scent of jasmine teased his senses, and he studied her hair a moment, wondering if that was why she smelled so damn good.

"You dance very well, Mr. Armstrong. I suspect you had dance lessons as a young man."

He'd had dance lessons for a lot longer than that. As a duke's son, no child of his father would be lacking in ballroom etiquette or grace. He'd known how to dance and dance well since he was in short coats. "I do try to ensure I never tread on any of my partner's toes. I hope not to disappoint you, Miss Clare."

She glanced up at him, their gazes clashed, and for the life of him, he could not look away. Her eyes, sharp and quick, watched him with utter conviction. He realized he never wanted to be looked upon any other way from Molly.

"Now, I only have to fear that I shall tread on yours. I do hope that is not the case," she said, laughing a little at her quip.

She was all womanly curves, tempting and a stark reminder of all that he'd lost by fleeing to Rome all those years ago. Had he stayed in London, there was little doubt that he would have married by now. Settled down with a woman such as the one in his arms and had a handful of children. He'd always wanted a family, his father had been loving, and he wanted to be just like his sire.

Hugh sighed and concentrated on the dance, not wanting to dwell on the past. He wanted to enjoy himself and give Molly a pleasant evening that was just as enjoyable as her day was.

"You have proven yourself to be just as apt at dancing as me. Why these last two turns about the room, and you have not injured my feet once."

"I confess, I too have had many years of practice. I'm sure it will not surprise you to know that I'm not a woman in her first season. I'm eight and twenty. At that age, I do believe I could become a master of dancing and give instruction."

Hugh pulled her close as he guided them about a turn at one end of the room. The atrium ballroom was a crush, beeswax candles lay within the sconces on the wall, making the makeshift ballroom magical.

"You are not ancient at eight and twenty, Molly. If we're declaring our ages, I must advise you that I'm two and thirty. I hope you do not think that too old for a woman such as yourself." Hugh glanced over Molly's head, not wanting to see if she was shocked or delighted by his words. Words that he'd not thought to utter. He would need to be better behaved before he did say something that had her packing her bags and heading back to England.

"Isn't it always gentlemen who believe women of my age are too old to be of use to them? Men, it would seem, have the luxury of being any grand age to make an equally grand match. Women, on the other hand, if they are not married within a year or two of their coming out, are termed old maids and too long in the tooth to do anything but be shipped off to the country to be a caregiver for either their parents or their sibling's children."

The thought was not a pleasant one, but Molly was right. Society could be cruel and unfair to women. "Well, I shall not let anyone ship you off to the country, my dear. Not at least while you're here in Rome with me in any case. I shall keep you safe from purgatory."

She studied him a moment. Hugh met her gaze, and a punch in his nether region would have been less injuring. There was something about the woman in his arms that he relished. She made him think of things, of home and building a home, of children, while another part of her made him crave.

Made the rogue he'd once been when he'd had the freedom to do whatever he liked—before his brother's demand had made him vilified by his peers—want to slip out of the dance, hide somewhere in this Roman villa and kiss her until the sun came up.

"You're quite the gentleman, and I thank you. If I am to travel out in the country, I do hope you'll accompany me. I should imagine you have seen many wonderful things in this country that a tourist such as myself may not know about."

He could, he supposed, convey her down to Naples and show her his country estate. Hugh could picture her now

37

standing on the balcony that housed the ancient city's views beyond, the warm Mediterranean sun and sea air teasing her unblemished skin and sweet figure.

"It would be my honor to show you a little more of Italy if that is your wish. Simply tell me when you would like to go, and I shall arrange it."

"Really?" she asked him, surprise blossoming on her features and making her even more beautiful than she already was.

His hand flexed about her hip, and he wished he could steal her away now. He coveted that what he was feeling about the woman in his arms was reciprocated.

Hugh steeled himself to finish the dance less he make a fool of himself with a woman he'd only known a day. It was only because bedmates had been absent from his life of late. His life in London had also plagued him, memories of everything he'd given up by agreeing to his brother's demands taunting him of what he'd lost.

Now that he was the duke, he supposed he no longer had to hide away in Rome. He could return to London and take up his place in society. His mother had passed some years ago. His sister certainly would welcome him back, and he needed to be in England to support her.

But he could not. They had turned their back on him, and now he would never return home. Out of spite or pride he could not say, but England and the society he once graced could go to the devil. Which would mean that after Molly's four weeks in Rome, he would have to say goodbye to her as well.

The latter impending day did not sit well with him. It was a day not to be borne.

CHAPTER 5

They returned home from the ball in the early hours of the morning. The impending dawn glowed bright on the eastern horizon, some of Rome's buildings already turning from dusky gray to a warmer shade of sandstone.

They walked through the courtyard in silence, Mr. Armstrong's warm, large hand on the small of her back, leaving her breathless and flushed. He'd been so very attentive all evening, so very handsome and sweet.

A woman could fall for a gentleman like Hugh.

A smile quirked her lips as they stepped into the atrium, a lone, male servant asleep on the chair near the door. "May I escort you to your room, Molly?"

"Thank you," she said, starting up the stairs, the sound of her name on his lips warming her blood. Molly's skin prickled, all too aware of the tall, muscular figure walking beside her. She had not thought to meet any gentleman while in Rome. This was a holiday purely to enjoy the sights of Italy. It was indeed a fortunate turn of events that Mr. Armstrong had arrived in her life. Ava had mentioned very little about Hugh, she had never met the gentleman, and had assured Molly that he was away from the city for the duration of her stay.

How very fortunate she was that he'd come back and decided to stay. Her trip to Rome already in the day she'd spent with him had been tremendous, and she hoped just the start of many more to come.

They came up to the door to her room, and she paused, turning to face him, having to glance up due to his towering height. "Thank you for the wonderful night. I shall treasure it always. I cannot remember the last time I had so much fun."

His lips quirked into a grin, his eyes inviting and warm. "The pleasure was all mine, Molly." He leaned down, the brush of his lips against her cheek making her breath catch. Should she turn just the littlest bit, their lips would meet. The scent of sandalwood teased her senses, and unwittingly she reached out, clasping his upper arms. Strong, toned muscles met her fingers, and she had the overwhelming urge to squeeze his flesh, see if it was indeed as strong as it felt beneath her fingers.

He pulled back, watching her. Time stood still. Her stomach fluttered when he didn't move away. She could kiss him if she wished. Did she want to? Did he?

Oh yes, yes she did, very much. His gaze dipped to her mouth, and liquid heat pooled at her core. Her breath hitched, she fumbled for the door handle, pushing herself into her room, and away from temptation. "Thank you again, Hugh, for the pleasant evening. Goodnight," she said, not waiting for his reply before she closed the door.

She stood there a moment, forcing herself not to move, not to wrench open the door and jerk him into her arms, taking from him what he was so obviously offering.

The sound of retreating footsteps sounded in the hall outside, and she breathed out a relieved sigh. She couldn't throw herself at him. They were starting to be friends. He was going to be showing her about Rome some more and the surrounding countryside. She could not jeopardize any of that. She wouldn't. Her time here was so precious, to start a love affair with a man she would not marry would be the worst decision she could ever make.

Her cousin played that game of giving herself to someone before wedding vows were spoken and had paid for her error of judgment with her life. She would not be another silly chit to be fooled by a handsome face and sweet words.

No matter how alluring that may be.

～

*T*he following day Hugh was impatient for her to visit the Vatican, and by the time she had broken her fast in her room and come downstairs, a carriage was waiting for them to take them to their morning location.

If he missed her at breakfast, he did not say, and nor was she willing to give an excuse as to why she had not ventured down. After their almost-kiss last night, embarrassment had kept her upstairs.

Why she was acting like a blushing debutante, she did not know. From Hugh's easy manner and charming self, he seemed oblivious to what had transpired between them.

"I shall ride on the box if you do not mind, Miss Clare," her companion said, smiling up at Mr. Armstrong's manservant, Marcus, who had already sat on the driver's seat.

Molly took in the secret little smile between the two and wondered if her companion, too, was embarking on her own adventure, one of her heart. "Of course, if you wish."

"If you need anything, do let me know. I will have Marcus stop the carriage."

"Miss Clare," Hugh said, holding out his hand to help her climb up in the equipage.

Molly braced herself to feel his touch and fought to school her features when her body thrummed at his presence, his voice, and warmth.

"Thank you." She swallowed her nerves and climbed up into the carriage, settling back onto the squabs and waiting for Hugh to join her.

The carriage dipped as he climbed inside, he rapped on the roof, and the carriage lurched forward.

His usual affable self, he seemed pleased to be with her again, no hint as to what had transpired between them in the early hours of the morning clouding his opinion of her. It was as if all was forgotten or was only imagined in Molly's mind.

This was for the best, of course. Molly did not need him to think that there could be anything else between them other than friendship. Unless, of course, she fell in love with him and he offered for her hand. Then, and only then, would she be willing even to contemplate giving herself to the gentleman.

Dressed in tan, buckskin breeches and highly polished black hessian boots, he again looked like a gentleman ready to stroll about Hyde Park. His white shirt had a loose cravat tied in the barrel knot design and a tan jacket. No waistcoat. No hat. No gloves. Not overly formal, which seemed to suit him. Not that he needed much clothing to look the epitome of sophistication, she would gather he need wear nothing at all, and he'd be perfect in her opinion.

Heat brushed her cheeks, and she took an interest in the streets passing them by outside the window.

"You shall like the Sistine Chapel, Molly. The paintings on the ceiling are simply unforgettable."

Excitement thrummed through her veins, not only because of their destination but because they were alone. How fortunate it was that Miss Sinclair had taken a liking to Marcus, and if the manservant's sweet smile back at her companion was anything to go by, he liked her also.

"I cannot thank you enough for taking me about, Hugh. I shall tell Ava and Whitstone of your kindness to me while I was here."

He threw her a small smile, glancing out the window. "It is a shame that you're only here for such a short amount of time. I feel like I shall miss you when you return to England. It has been so very long that I've had a little part of home beneath my roof. The last time it was Whitstone himself who had come to visit, and you being a mutual friend of His Grace, I know that I can trust you with such declarations."

Molly reached out and took his gloveless hand, squeezing it a little. "I should imagine it is very hard to be so far away from your home. Do you think you shall ever return to England? I know I should look forward to seeing you again."

"I will never return, no." A muscle worked in his jaw, and he frowned, staring at something outside the carriage window. "Rome is my home now, and this is where I shall stay. But," he said, placing his hand over hers that she realized was still laying atop his, "you are always more than welcome to stay anytime you wish."

"If only I could, but my family could not afford to send me for too long. If it were not for my friends, I would not have been able to make my dream a reality. I could not impose on you for any more length of time than I plan on doing already."

"Nonsense. I would more than welcome you to stay, whenever and however long you like."

"We're already skirting on impropriety with me under your roof and you in residence. I do not think I wish to push my fortune too far, sir."

His hand lifted hers a little, and he started to play with her fingers, tracing them with his own through her kid-leather gloves. "You should take these off. It is too warm for gloves in Rome."

Without waiting for a response, he flicked open the two little buttons on her wrist, his bare fingers slipping under her glove to pull her hand free of the soft leather. Fresh air hit her flesh, and he was right, it was cooler not wearing them.

He turned her fingers over, inspecting them. "You have lovely hands."

Molly looked at her gloveless hand encased in his. It looked small and delicate against his large, tanned one. She'd never really paid much heed to her hands, but perhaps he was right. They were certainly not awful-looking.

"You have large, strong hands." The words slipped from her lips, and as much as she may wish to take them back, she could not. It was an absurd notion, but she'd already spent too much time thinking about his hands and what they would feel like caressing her flesh.

Nice, very nice indeed.

The carriage turned, and Hugh moved to the side of the equipage, taking stock of their location. "We're nearly there. Should we be fortunate, we may get a glimpse of a cardinal or the Pope himself. Would you like that?"

"Oh, very much, although I'm no longer so very religious, I still respect those who are. Are you catholic, Hugh?"

He grinned, shaking his head. "No, protestant, and you?"

"The same." She moved over to the window and, pulling the leather strap, lowered the glass. Molly leaned out of the carriage, looking straight ahead and gasped. An imposing, Renaissance building met her vision, complete with a large dome atop it, columns and ornamental statues adorned the building, giving it an air of grandeur she'd never seen before. The carriage rumbled up the long road, gaining ever closer to the circular square. The buildings that circled the Vatican City faced this large square, and people milled about in the area, taking in the magnificent sights.

"I feel that I'm going to enjoy our outing today," she said as the carriage rocked to a halt, and Marcus opened the carriage door.

Hugh jumped out, reaching back to take her hand to help her alight. "You will be amazed, I'm certain. So many people never get to see such gifts. This will truly be a day you will never forget."

Molly couldn't help but smile at Hugh's words. There was little doubt that the day already was one never to forget. Hugh placed her hand atop his arm, turning to face his driver and her companion. "Please come back to collect us here in St. Peters Square in a couple of hours."

"There are plenty of people about, Miss Sinclair. You may return to the villa." Her companion beamed at Marcus, and it solidified Molly's curiosity. There was most certainly something up between the two people.

The driver tipped his hat as Marcus climbed back onto the box. "Of course, Mr. Armstrong."

Molly didn't spare the carriage a second glance as it turned and rumbled down the gravel road. Instead, her attention was caught and held by the magnificent buildings before her. They started toward St. Peter's Basilica, it's large, imposing dome looking down on the populace below. From the abundance of people, it seemed to be the most popular structure to visit.

"We shall go to the Sistine Chapel through St. Peter's Basilica. I want you to see the nave."

Excitement thrummed through Molly. She was in Rome, at Vatican City, and with a gentleman she'd not thought to have met. He was a wonderful host and guide, and she could not thank Ava and Whitstone enough that they were friends with Mr. Armstrong.

They walked up a line of steps heading toward the entrance to the large church. They passed under six high columns before stepping into the portico and then the nave. The gold and ornate columns were unlike anything Molly had seen before. Marble, sculptures, and murals were a feast to one's eye. She could not take it all in, the size alone was tremendous, so many details and history that it would take a person years to view each and every-thing under the grand roof and view its beauty.

"This is overwhelming. I always thought Westminster and St. Pauls were beautiful, but this is another beast altogether."

Hugh chuckled, walking them leisurely up the middle

of the nave, he too looking about the great space. "It's a feast for any historian or antiquities collector. You can understand why so many people come to admire this church."

"Oh yes," she said, squeezing his arm a little. "Take me to the Sistine Chapel. I cannot wait any longer."

He nodded slightly. "I'm at your service, Miss Clare." He pulled her back out into the portico and, turning left, they headed up some stairs before turning left again and climbing stairs that worked their way up one side of a building separate to St. Peter's Basilica.

"I had always thought the chapel was part of the church. From where you're taking me, this is not the case?" she asked, staring ahead to the door that loomed before them.

"It's a chapel off to the side and separate. I did not know this either until I visited for the first time. I'm glad I have a companion who appreciates history and beauty as much as I do."

She met his gaze as they made the top landing, and she beamed at him, her body thrumming with expectation. "I'm delighted you're here with me too. Had I done this alone or with Miss Sinclair, who dislikes travel and anything different to what she is used to, it would not have been the same. Thank you for escorting me, Mr. Armstrong. You're truly a good man."

"I wouldn't go that far, Miss Clare." His laugh held an edge of mocking, and she wondered at it. He was a good man and had been a wonderful friend to her these past days.

"I would," she disagreed as they walked through a small door into a rectangular room full of painted murals. Molly bit her lip, speechless by what she saw.

"Michelangelo, for all that he proclaimed to be a sculptor and not a painter, certainly had talent when he held a brush."

Gaping, Molly closed her mouth with a snap, arching her neck to look upon the roof that she'd read so many books on, but had never beheld in life. The famous making of Adam stared down upon them, grand and celebrated. She blinked back tears at finally being here, at seeing this treasure from a master of art.

"Beautiful, isn't it?" she said, swiping at her cheek and yet not embarrassed by the fact she was emotional before Hugh. One could not look at such art and not be moved, to be indifferent to what adorned the walls could only mean the person had no soul.

"I quite agree," he whispered.

Molly glanced at Hugh and found him staring at her, his eyes heavy with an emotion she did not recognize. She tore her gaze away, calming her racing heart. This was not the place for her to throw herself at him. They were friends, he did not mean anything by his words, merely that the paintings were beautiful. Not that she was.

She stepped forward, taking in the images of the popes drawn on a higher level of the room, of the arched windows and floor that was some sort of mosaic of a circular pattern, seemingly more modern than the historical room and paintings that stood within.

They studied the paintings for some time, a guide coming over to them and telling them a little of the painting's meanings, of how long it took Michelangelo to paint the room.

Several hours passed before they exited St. Peter's Basilica, their carriage waiting patiently outside The Square. "Are you pleased that you traveled thousands of miles to see Rome and all of this?" Hugh asked, pulling her close to his side as they strode across The Square.

Molly breathed deep, feeling at home in this city, this country. Although she had friends that she adored and loved in England, they were all married now, on paths of their own. Her family no longer circulated in town, not after what happened to her cousin. Even though they never circulated in the sphere in which her friends now enjoyed, it still allowed Molly to have her family in London and not be isolated.

She was alone quite a lot now that Evie had married and moved out of the townhouse they once shared with Willow.

Molly pulled Hugh to a stop. He glanced down at her, a small frown line between his brow marring his perfect visage. This close, she could admire his long obsidian eyelashes, the slight shadow of stubble across his cheeks and jaw. An ache thrummed deep in her belly, and for the first time in her life, she acted upon her feelings.

Her fingers slid up behind the lapels on his coat. She clasped them tight, pulling Hugh close before leaning up and kissing him in the middle of St. Peter's Square.

Molly ignored the gasps from those passing them by and viewing their public display of affection, but she did not stop. His lips were as soft as silk just as she imagined them to be. His arms wrapped about her waist, pulling her close, and he deepened the kiss. taking her mouth in a kiss like she'd never imagined before. His tongue slipped into her mouth, and she gasped, having not expected such intimacy when she'd started this foray into passion.

The sensation was unlike anything she'd ever experienced, but she liked it. Liked having him kiss her with abandon and without care of who saw them. They were in

Rome, after all. The eternal city that had seen millions of love affairs just like the one she was embarking on.

Molly held on to his shoulders, mimicking him as much as she could. Her first kiss was all heat and deliciousness, and she couldn't get enough. She never wanted to stop kissing him.

He reached up, clasping her face with his hands. He tipped her head a little, and the world stopped spinning. At this angle, somehow, he made her open to him like a flower, blooming from his warmth. Before she knew what she was about, she slid her tongue against his, marveling at the friction.

Hugh moaned, his hands spiking into her hair as he wrenched her closer. His body, hard against hers, made her breath hitch, her most private of places ache. Their kiss turned desperate. Distantly, as if a million miles away, she could feel her hair unraveling under his onslaught. She cared little. All she heeded was this sweet, kind, virile, handsome man who was kissing her within an inch of her life.

The sound of a gentleman clearing his throat nearby impinged on their kiss, and Hugh pulled back, staring at her as if he didn't know who it was in his arms. Molly refused to glance about to see who was watching, judging them. They could all go to hades as far as she was concerned.

"That was..." he said, his words breathless against her lips.

"It was, wasn't it?" She grinned and stepped out of his hold. Molly took his hand and started toward the carriage. Her hair fell about her shoulders, and she didn't try to fix it before they made the carriage. There was little point. Half her pins were scattered about St. Peter's Square, after all.

Along with her reputation should anyone have recognized her.

*H*ugh helped Molly up into the carriage and followed her inside, slamming the door behind him to mask his shaking hands. Damn it all to hell. What had just happened? Never in his life had he ever acted in such a scandalous way. And in St. Peter's Square to boot. The Pope would disapprove should he have seen such a public kiss between two people not even married.

What had he been thinking?

As to that, not a lot. Nothing at all except how perfect Molly felt in his arms. How her sweet, soft lips felt pressed up against his and how much he wanted to feel them again.

Right now.

He pulled the blinds down in the carriage, giving them privacy. "You kissed me, Molly. Does that mean you want to kiss me again?"

Her eyes flew wide with alarm, and he grinned, marveling at how she could kiss him with such sweet abandon and then be shocked when asked about it. How adorable was this woman and how much would he miss her when she left?

"I like you," she stated, matter-of-fact, her hands clasped tight in her lap. "I never kissed a man before, you see, and after the wonderful day we've just had, well..." She paused, glancing at something in her lap, those sweet lips she'd just kissed him with clasped tight between her teeth, driving him to distraction. He gripped the seat, forcing himself to remain where he was and not move. Not molest her again in the carriage this time when there was no one to stop them.

"Well," she continued. "I decided that I wanted it to be you whom I kissed. You're probably going to be the only man I ever kiss, and so I took what I wanted. I do apologize if I shocked or offended you."

Hugh chuckled, leaning back in the squabs. She met his gaze, and he hoped she could read in his eyes that he was far from offended. Aroused, intrigued...yes. But offended? Hell no.

"Let me tell you, Molly, that you have my permission to kiss me whenever you desire. I've not been with a woman for some time, and your company these last few days has been a sweet elixir to my soul. A stolen kiss or two will hurt no one, especially me."

Her cheeks bloomed into a pretty rose hue, and he shifted to sit beside her, reaching up to brush her hair back behind her ear. "I'm glad you kissed me because I've wanted to kiss you from the moment I saw you in my atrium, in your pretty blue gown and excited about seeing Rome for the first time."

"Really?" A smile blossomed on her lips, and he couldn't help but grin back. "So I can kiss you whenever I like?"

He nodded. "I wouldn't be a gentleman if I did not suggest that if we're to kiss again that it should be in private. Perhaps St. Peter's Square is not the best location, but a carriage with the blinds drawn, well, no one will see us here."

"That is true." Molly glanced about the coach, her inspection taking in the lowered blinds. "I want to kiss you again. Am I not scandalous?"

"A little," he teased. "But so am I, so we're a good

match." Hugh didn't wait for her to initiate the kiss this time. Instead, he seized her sweet face and kissed her, deep and sure. Their tongues tangled, heat licking his skin, his cock aching for her touch. He'd not reacted to a woman in such a way ever in his life. He wanted to make her crave him as much as he feared he would covet her when she left.

Her arms tangled about his neck, her breasts, full and heavy, sat against his chest. His hands itched to clasp a handful of the voluptuous flesh. To tease and pinch her nipples, he was certain would be puckered little knobs inside her dress.

The thought of licking, kissing her there, sent a bolt of desire to his cock. "You're so sweet. I cannot get enough of you," he gasped against her lips.

She stared back at him, her eyes cloudy with desire, her lips swollen from his touch. "And I, you."

Hugh took her lips again, hoisting her up against his person. Her stomach sat against his engorged cock. He wasn't sure what she would think of him, or his reaction to her, but when she undulated against him, sliding her sweet body to tease his, the world's axis tipped.

It took all his self-control not to slide his hand down her back, clasp a nice handful of her ass and grind against her. She moved closer still, pushing him back against the window, her untutored kiss before becoming more proficient with each passing moment. Molly was a quick learner. If he weren't careful, she would undo him in the carriage like a green lad who'd never touched a woman before.

The carriage rocked to a halt, and with a jerk, he sat them up. "We're home." The word home reverberated about in his mind. The Roman villa was certainly his home, but he liked having Molly under its roof and being part of his life. To take someone about, a little slice of home that he vowed not to miss, soothed the beast that roared inside that hated what his family had done. Having Molly here reminded him of everything that he'd lost because of them. The possibility of a future. A wife as passionate and sweet as his houseguest was. Perhaps even Molly herself.

She sat up, adjusting her gown and addressing her hair as best as she could before the door opened, and Marcus set down the steps for them.

Hugh jumped down, turning about to help her alight. Her fingers enclosed within his and a bolt of awareness shot up his arm. He took a calming breath, pushing down the ache in his chest at the realization that she would be leaving in only a few short weeks. He wasn't so certain that he wanted her to leave at all.

If he could, he'd keep her for himself. Forever.

CHAPTER 6

The following day Molly toured the markets of Piazza Navona with Miss Sinclair, along with Hugh's manservant escorting her since Hugh had to address some missives from England that had arrived the day before when they were at the Vatican.

Molly picked up some flowers from one of the stalls and a collection of gifts that she would take back to England for her friends. One vendor was selling little porcelain statues of famous gladiators of ancient Rome. Hallie would love these, especially since she was so very fond of history.

They strolled the markets for some time, breaking their fast at a stall that sold bread and dried meats. Molly had never eaten in public like this before, and it was a marvel, a liberating feeling. She could get used to being a Roman citizen, especially if she were fortunate enough to return home to the villa and see Hugh each day.

The thought of him sent her stomach to catapult into a thousand circles. After their kiss in St. Peter's Square and then in the carriage on the way home, she had thought they would dine and spend time with each other for the evening, but Hugh had received a mountain of letters that even this morning was taking up his time. Stopping him from accompanying her today.

They made their way back to the carriage, Marcus carrying her parcels for her. Miss Sinclair had seemed to have a change of heart regarding the city and travel. She was all smiles and compliments on their outing. Marcus was a positive influence on her.

As she waited for the parcels to be hitched, her mind turned to Hugh. What was the business that was so very important that he'd been unavailable last evening and today? Perhaps he still had business dealings in London that needed taking care of. She had been monopolizing his time somewhat since he'd offered to take her about Rome. It was only expected that he would have to decline and stay home to complete his work some days.

Molly climbed up in the carriage, nodding to Miss Sinclair as she pulled off her bonnet, wiping her brow with her lace handkerchief. "What an enjoyable morning. However, I fear a megrim is settling in."

"If you're feeling poorly, I'll have Maria bring up a tisane for you. Will you be dining with the servants, or would you prefer to dine in your room?"

"I should not leave you alone with Mr. Armstrong as much as I have, Miss Clare. My duty is to keep you safe. It is already terribly scandalous that we're staying under his roof with him in residence. I just hope the news does not beat us back to London. Your reputation will be ruined."

Molly glanced out the window, grinning at Miss Sinclair's words. Her reputation was already ruined had anyone seen their kiss yesterday in the square and recognized them. She could not regret it, however. Her first kiss had been given freely to Mr. Armstrong, and from the moment he'd kissed her back, she knew that her bold actions had been the right thing to do.

"We know so very little about him, Miss Clare. I would hate to have your reputation ruined by not doing my duty as your chaperone."

"I'm eight and twenty, Miss Sinclair. No one cares what I do or how I go about. You forget what it was like for me in London. Other than my friends, no one cared about me at all. I was not titled nor rich, practically invisible."

"I do not think your parents would agree, Miss Clare. Think of your cousin. She was lured in by a pretty face and false promises. I do not want to see the same happen to you, and God knows, Mr. Armstrong has a face akin to wickedness. What a handsome man, and one who knows how to use such looks, I'm sure, when the need arises."

Molly chuckled, unable to disagree with her companion's summations. "A pretty face will not fool me, but even so, Mr. Armstrong is a gentleman and has been very kind to me. But I promise you, Miss Sinclair, that I shall not do anything that will harm my family or myself. I will not make the same mistake as Laura."

"He promised her marriage, Miss Clare. She thought herself in love."

"I know what Laura thought." Molly knew firsthand what her cousin had been promised, and the heartache her friend had gone through before her son's birth. The death of them both only a few days later had left the family scarred and cautious.

Lord Farley, the Duke of St. Albans's younger brother, was a fiend who did not deserve to breathe as far as Molly was concerned. If only she could tell the prig to his face that she hated him, that what he'd done had ruined her friend and her future.

Had caused irreparable damage to the family that they struggled to this day to live with.

Molly wasn't naïve enough not to know Laura too was at fault, she had allowed things to go too far between them before they were married, but still, when one falls in love, she could see how very difficult it would be to deny oneself what one desired.

Just as she now desired Mr. Armstrong above anyone else. He could be her downfall, the man who made her want to throw all caution aside and simply live, love, and play to her heart's content.

As much as she did not understand her cousin's emotions or what made her do the things she had done with Lord Farley, she could understand them now. After kissing Hugh, she could understand the desires of the heart were sometimes too great to resist.

The carriage rocked to a halt before the villa, and Miss Sinclair continued to look displeased with her. "He's taken a fancy to you. The staff can see it as plain as day, and so can I. He's a man, his risk is nothing to yours. Please keep your head about yourself when with him. That is all I ask."

Molly reached across the seat and clasped Miss Sinclair's hand. Her anxiety on Molly's behalf doing her character and position justice. "Mr. Armstrong's attentions will not injure me, I promise. He's an honorable man. I may be a little long in the tooth, but I think he's genuine. He'll not play with my heart unless he intends to keep it for himself. There is hope yet, Miss Sinclair that I may have found my match."

Molly smiled and turned to alight from the vehicle. The villa door stood ajar, and inside the home's walls stood

Hugh, waiting for her in the afternoon sun. His shirt was free from his tan breeches, the arms rolled up about his elbows and showing off his golden-hue skin and muscular forearms.

Butterflies took flight in her stomach, and she stifled a sigh of delight at the sight of him. How could a man that she'd only known a few days be so consuming? Make her feel like a green girl experiencing her first Season and being courted by London's most handsome man.

She walked up to him, unable to stop the smile that formed on her lips. "Good afternoon, Mr. Armstrong. I hope you had a productive day as you'd hoped."

He guided her over to a part of the garden that housed a small marble alcove and bench. Vines grew above the seat, giving the occupants privacy. Molly sat, pulling her shawl about her shoulders as the temperature in the hidden niche was cooler than in the courtyard.

"I was able to finish what needed attending, but I could not concentrate."

"Really?" Molly frowned up at him. He sat beside her, the side of his leg touching hers. Her skin prickled in awareness, and she took a calming breath, needing to control herself and her reactions to him. He did not need to know that she liked him perhaps more than she ought to like a man she hardly knew. "Why could you not concentrate?"

He reached out, sliding his thumb across her bottom lip, and she leaned into him, wanting more of his touch. To have his thumb replaced with his lips. "I could not concentrate because I knew you were walking about Rome without me. I fear that you can never return to London as I'll miss you too much."

His sweet words made a pang of regret and panic take

flight inside her. She could not stay, not unless he offered marriage, but she was unsure if he asked whether she could live so far away from her friends and family. Even with the intoxicating, consuming man that was slowly taking her heart and making it his.

"You tease," she said, making light of his words and not wanting to face just what they did mean, what they could imply for both of them.

He shook his head, closing the space between them. "No, I'm not. I've never been more honest."

The moment his lips touched hers, Molly was lost. She gave herself to his kiss that turned demanding and wicked, and unlike the other kisses they'd shared so far. This one took her breath away. His hand spiked into her hair, making her gasp. The moment she did, he took advantage and thrust his tongue against hers, pulling her into a world of desire, needs, and wants.

Her body ached for his touch. She clasped his side, anchoring herself lest she float away and never return to her body. Faintly, she was aware of his other hand, sliding up her waist. A moan burst free when it covered her breast, kneading the aching flesh. His thumb and forefinger found her nipple. He rolled it through the fabric of her dress, and she moaned.

She crossed her legs as she leaned against him, trying to appease the deep, thrumming ache between her legs. It did not help. She wanted him to touch her there as well. To tease and kiss her and bring that desire to heel.

"You're the sweetest woman. It is confirmed you must stay. Forget London and stay here with me."

Molly pulled back, hoping he was playing while a little of her wished she could be so brave. "You'll have to convince me harder than this, Hugh."

"Hmm," he said, grinning at her, his chiseled jaw and high cheekbones reminiscent of the many statues of gods that littered Rome. "Is that a challenge, Miss Clare?"

Molly stood, pulling him to stand before starting back toward the villa. "It most certainly is. Change my mind, and we'll see."

"I will win, you know. I'm very persuasive."

She chuckled, not caring that Miss Sinclair stood on the balcony above and saw their interaction or the closeness of their friendship. She had not done anything so very wrong. A kiss was not the end of her reputation or the end of the world. And it was not like Miss Sinclair was not embarking on a love affair of her own. "We shall see, will we not?"

"We will," he said, kissing her hand and throwing her a wink.

CHAPTER 7

*L*ate that evening, a knock sounded on her bedroom door and, having dismissed Miss Sinclair some hours before, Molly slid from atop her bed where she had been reading, placing the book down before seeing who was there.

She cracked the door but an inch and fought back the urge to grin like a silly nincompoop. "Mr. Armstrong. Is anything wrong?" she asked, opening the door farther and checking up and down the hall that there was no emergency he was waking her for.

"Not at all. I wanted to show you something in the villa that I have recently had restored. I think you shall enjoy it."

"Really?" Intrigued, Molly stepped out into the hall and shut her door. Hugh held out his arm, and she took it willingly, any excuse to touch him, and she would. When she returned to London, she would miss him dreadfully.

After they had dined together, her mind had raced all evening with what he could mean by trying to persuade her to stay. Did he intend to ask her to marry him? If he did, would she say yes? Molly glanced at him quickly, knowing full well the answer to her question. Oh yes, she would marry him without a second thought.

Even knowing him so little, he made her blood sing, her body yearn and no one, not in all the years she'd treaded the ballroom floors in London, had reacted so to a man.

They made their way through the villa through the atrium and out into the courtyard. Sconces burned against the villa's walls and lanterns lit the garden paths, lighting their way. They headed in the direction of a room that had an oiled wooden door leading into it. Many such rooms ran about the villa walls, and Molly was yet to see what was in those spaces, but this one's door looked repaired and varnished.

"It's inside here." He turned to watch her a moment, and before she knew what he was about, he stole a kiss. Molly tried to make it linger, but instead, he grinned, turned, and threw the door open.

Molly gasped, stepping into the warm, tiled room that had an arched ceiling. She could not believe what she was seeing. It was as if she were stepping back two millennia to Roman times. The room held two deep, tiled pools in the center of the space, sconces burned on each wall, and what looked to be steam coming up from one of the pools made the water inviting.

"Is this a bathhouse?" she queried, taking in the painted mosaics on the wall that although were new, were of scantily clad men and women enjoying baths such as the ones that sat before them.

"It is. Rome used to have hundreds of them as you would know, and this villa had a derelict, ruined one when I bought it. I've had it restored and have had the hypocaust under the floors cleaned out and rebuilt. The hot air that flows beneath the caldarium or hot bath is heated by coal and warms the floor and water. The frigidarium or cold bath I put in myself, the room did not have one. This bath was located in the room next door, but I needed space for servants' quarters and so placed it in here as well. But of course, there is no heating system beneath this bath."

He took her hand, pulling her toward the steaming-hot bath. "I thought you might like to bathe. Alone, of course," he said, grinning wickedly and making her body hum. "You may use the room whenever you like."

Molly didn't know a great deal about history and had learned much more from listening to Hallie and her many travels. However, one thing she did know about Roman baths was what happened to the person after they bathed. "You do not have a servant who rubs you down with oils after your bath, Mr. Armstrong?" Molly couldn't help but chuckle at her teasing. For a moment, Hugh looked a little shocked by her words.

"I do not. No." He moved over to a nearby daybed that sat in one corner, sitting on its edge. "I can arrange that for you, however, if that is what you wish."

Molly joined him, standing before him. He glanced up at her, his long locks mussed with a little curl. He looked vulnerable all of a sudden, and something in her chest ached. She reached out, running her hands over his unshaven jaw, reveling in the feel of his short whiskers. "Are you trying to tempt me to stay in Rome with this bath that I have at my disposal whenever I wish?"

He shrugged, a teasing grin upon his lips. "Is it working?"

Molly looked over her shoulder at the water. The bath looked deep and clean, and so appetizingly warm. It had been so very hot in Rome, and she would revel in bathing. She went over to the bath, looking over her shoulder and meeting Hugh's gaze. He was watching her, a hungry light in his eyes that made her stomach clench. She wanted him to look at her like he wanted to consume her and gorge on every piece of her body. The thought of him, kissing her the way he did in the carriage, of having him take her, left her aching.

Perhaps she ought to jump in the cool bath instead. All his deliciousness was making her discombobulated.

"Can you help me with my buttons?"

His eyes flashed with need, and without hesitation, he stood, striding toward her like a Roman warrior heading to war. Molly looked at the water, steeling herself for his touch on her back. And then it was there, the slip of his fingers upon her gown. He made short work of the buttons that ran down her back.

As the last button on her gown let go, Molly brought up her hands to clasp the front of her dress. Hugh did not stop there. His fingers slid down atop her bottom, the tug of the drawstrings on her corset making her wobble. She bit her lip and closed her eyes, forcing herself not to turn around. Should she do so, she would be lost, and she could not do that. For as much as she had come to realize that she wanted Hugh, wanted him to want her to stay, possibly marry her if that was where he thought their friendship was heading, she could not give herself unless the words were spoken.

At least she did not have the worry that he was merely a wealthy lord looking for a little entertainment while she was in Rome. His being untitled suited her, and she liked that he was a self-made man, had not inherited his fortune from his parents.

"What is it that you do here in Rome, Mr. Armstrong? You have not told me."

His fingers slipped between the laces, working their way up her back. "I grow wine on my country estate here in Italy, and I dabble in the shipping of goods back and forth from India and England. I've been fortunate that I'm not beholden to anyone, and I live a comfortable life here in Rome."

"Your parents, are they still alive?" Not that she wanted to intrude or seem ungracious, but she was curious. For as much as she longed to turn about and crawl into his arms and stay there forever, they did not know much about each other's lives. If she were to stay in Rome, if he did happen to ask for her hand, they ought to know everything there was to know.

"No, unfortunately, my father passed some years ago and my mother more recently. I was not there for her passing, not that she would wish for me to be."

Molly frowned, a pang of sadness swamping her at the pain she heard in his voice. She turned, staring up at him and wishing she could make the memories of his parents happy ones, just as hers were for her own.

"You were not close? I'm sorry if you were not."

He sighed, running a hand over his jaw before striding toward the door. "I am not. My mother made it clear when I left England that I was not needed or wanted there. I thought it would be contradictory to both our true feelings should I try and be there when she passed. I was correct when she wrote to me, telling me she did not regret her decision of years before."

For all of Hugh's words, there was something within his eyes, a pain hidden from those around him. He was not as immune to this hurt as he stated. The tightness of his mouth told her that no matter what his mother had said, her child had wished it otherwise. He wanted his mother's love, just as all children do, whether they receive it or not.

"I'm sorry, Hugh. That could not have been easy."

He grinned, the wicked and teasing gentleman once more. "What is not easy, my dear, is leaving you alone in this bathhouse to bathe without me. If you think my soul is tortured, it is, but only because of you and not because of a parent who may have had two sons, but only required one."

*H*ugh shut the door on the bathhouse and forced his legs to move toward the villa. The sanctuary of his tablinum. He supposed Molly would be curious about his past, his life when he lived in England. He'd not been prepared to answer such questions, not when he didn't want her to know he was the infamous Lord Hugh Farley, who had ruined a young debutante's life before fleeing to the continent.

Or so everyone thought.

Now the Duke of St. Albans, he supposed he could return to London, lift his nose to anyone who would naysay him, but it wasn't to be borne. He would not give the rats the gloating rights to curse his name and give him the cut direct. Not that they would. Not as one of the highest-ranking and wealthiest peers in England.

With the death of his mother and brother now too, all ability to clear his name was lost. There would be no redemption for him back in England, no matter how much he would like to return. To take up his duties for his father's sake, if no one else's, but he could not. His brother had ensured his name was mud.

Hugh strode into his library, closed the door, and went to the settee that sat before the unlit hearth, sinking into its plush cushions. With Molly intent on returning to England he would have to make a choice. Ask her to stay, to marry him, but therein itself was a problem. He could not marry her under false pretenses. Should he do so, any heirs they produced would not inherit his title, which left him with one choice.

To tell Molly the truth of who he is and the real reason he lived in Italy.

Unless, he could sign the marriage register in his real name without Molly being aware... Even so, he would have to check the legality of the marriage before any children were born.

What a conundrum.

He rubbed a hand over his jaw, the thought of admitting his lineage, his shame, not the feigned one his brother and mother had heaped on his head, but the shame of letting them force him to take the fall left a sour taste in his mouth.

Should he tell Molly the truth, he wasn't certain he could face the horror, the hurt that would shadow her pretty visage. He never wanted her to look at him as if she did not know who he was. To imagine her think him a cad who ruined a young woman's life was a shame he could not bear to see from her.

Why, however, was uncertain. They had known each other for such a short time, but the fire and the chemistry that burned between them were undeniable. Molly was a woman who had friends in high places. There would be little doubt in his mind that she would've heard of Miss Laura Cox and the wicked Lord Farley's ruination of her.

Hugh clasped his hands before his face, leaning on his

knees, staring at the blackened hearth in thought. He would be better off leaving her be. Stop all flirtation, all clandestine trips to the bathhouse such as the one tonight. Stop the stolen kisses in the carriage and merely become the host he was supposed to be. Or even better, leave Rome and return to his country estate near Naples. Remove himself from the temptation that was Molly.

He swore, throwing himself back into his chair. The idea of leaving Molly was no more palatable than telling her the truth and watching her leave for London. It was a hopeless case and one he would have to think upon more. Tonight he could not decide his course of action. What he could decide upon, however, was that he needed a stiff drink. Or perhaps, many.

CHAPTER 8

he following evening Molly once again stole down to the courtyard of the villa and snuck into the bathhouse. The room appeared prepared for use at any time, the sconces burned against the walls, the mosaic floor warm under her feet. Molly sighed, luxuriating in the most opulent space she'd ever experienced in her life.

Back in England at her family's small cottage, she had only ever bathed in a hip bath, and the one they had had not given her the ability to swim in warm, fragrant water. Whatever sweet flower oils they were putting in the water were delightful, and other than Hugh himself, she would miss this Roman bath more than anything else when she returned to England.

She had now been in Rome for almost a week, and so much had happened. Not only with her tours of the city, but here with Hugh. They had become friends instantly, and that attraction she felt for him had only grown with each moment she spent in his presence.

Today, however, he'd not been at the villa. The house-keeper had been at a loss as to his whereabouts.

Molly slipped off her robe and untied the small ribbon at the front of her shift, letting that too fall to the floor to pool at her feet. She sank into the water, careful not to slip on the steps before the warm bath engulfed her. Molly smiled, dipping under the water and swimming to the other end. She chuckled, knowing she was frolicking like some water nymph, and she was. Who would not when given such a gift of a Roman bath to use whenever they desired?

The door to the bathhouse opened, and she squealed, swimming to the side of the bath to stop Hugh from seeing her naked. He stumbled into the room and shut the door, seemingly oblivious to her being there.

"Hugh?" she asked. His head flicked up. His glassy eyes focused on her for the first time. Was he drunk?

"Molly," he panted. "I did not know you were in here. I thought everyone was abed."

"I was in bed," she started, watching as he moved over to a daybed, slumping down on the mattress. "But I grew hot and wanted to bathe. I thought it might help me sleep." She paused, watching him as he lay there, one arm slumped over his face, his legs off the side of the daybed as if he could not be bothered to lift them farther. "Are you well, Mr. Armstrong?"

"Do not call me Mr. Armstrong. Please."

He sounded tortured, ill even. Should she risk getting out and slipping on her clothes? He seemed to be only a minute or two away from sleeping. Her towel sat upon a nearby chair, but to clasp it, that too meant she would have to step out of the water completely to ensure her modesty was preserved.

Why had she not placed her towel closer to the bath?

"Are you well then, Hugh?" she asked again, moving along the side of the bath toward the steps.

"I am somewhat drunk, but not ill."

He seemed odd this evening. His words were hard and did not invite conversation. Was he angry at her? The reason for such a turn of character did not make sense. She had not seen him today and the last time they had spent time together, they had parted on good terms.

"What is it then?" she queried, wanting to know what ailed him.

"You."

"Me?" She stood on the bath floor, glancing at him over the side of the pool. He sat up, staring at her, and the desire that blazed in his ebony orbs fired her blood. It was dangerous for him to be in the room with her. She swallowed, her body tingling as his gaze dipped to her shoulders. Not that he could see beyond, but there was little doubt from his visage that he imagined what the rest of her looked like, naked and wet in the water.

"What have I done?" she queried when he didn't say anything further.

"You torment me."

Molly shut her mouth with a snap, unwilling to listen to such hogwash, and certainly unwilling to listen when he was foxed. She strode up the bath stairs, clasped her towel, and wrapped it about herself, ignoring the fact that her body burned. She could feel his attention upon her, scorching its way up and down her body as she covered herself with the soft linen.

Obscured enough to face him, she stalked over and stood a bare foot from his person. "I torment you. You sound like a petulant child. I have no more tormented you than you have me."

"Really?" He stood, towering over her. The breath in her lungs seized. His shirt was open, gaping far enough to see his chest and the scattering of hairs atop his skin.

Her mouth dried, her core ached.

"How do I torment you? Tell me."

His words, barely audible, were in themselves tormenting. His deep, throaty words made her yearn for more. Not just a stolen kiss, but a touch, caress, his hands pulling her against him so their bodies could take pleasure. There was little doubt in her mind that he could give her a lot of satisfaction. Her friends had been honest and open with her, telling her that she should not settle unless the gentleman who had taken her fancy made her burn.

She now understood those words, for burn she did. For him. She would not tell him how he made her feel. She would show him instead.

Her rules be damned.

*H*ugh wanted Molly with a need that he'd not expected to feel. His body was not itself. He ached every hour of every day, craved with an urgency that made his stomach churn. He needed her touch and her sweet, untutored kisses. She was all he thought about. A novelty he'd not experienced ever. But he was torn. What would she think of him when she found out the truth of his departure from England? Of what he was accused of?

Even if those accusations were incorrect, it did not change the fact that everyone thought it as truth. Miss Laura Cox was from a wealthy family, circulated in his social sphere. Even if her father wasn't titled, they were rich enough to be included in the nobility's social calendar. His brother had gone about his life in London after ruining Laura without a blink of an eye. Only too happy to ooh and ahh over the rumors, commiserate with his friends of his brother's downfall and atrocious behavior. A downfall that Henry should have faced instead of Hugh.

How was he to tell Molly of his past? To expect her to believe that he was innocent of the crime? It was his fault. He should never have agreed to take the fall. Should have told the truth and let his brother face the wrath of their peers. Laura, a sweet woman who he remembered being full of life and promise, had not deserved what she was meted out. His brother, having played with her emotions, should have offered for her hand, especially when Henry took her innocence and got her with child.

Henry had not. Instead, his brother had shunned her, watched from afar as the light in her eyes dimmed to a deathly gray. Ignored her until she no longer attended events and eventually left for the country. Hugh remembered the day his mother had received the missive from Miss Cox, demanding the Duke of St. Albans make good on his promise to marry her. That she would tell her father of his conduct if he did not do the right thing.

His mother had been enraged toward Laura. A fit of misplaced anger, as it should have been directed at her eldest son. From that point on, Henry ceased all communication with Miss Cox and explained that they did not take well to threats. That there was no proof that he was the father or that she had not given out her body to other gentlemen of their set.

That was when Hugh was asked to be the gentleman who had ruined her. To be the one to take the blame, so the head of the family's reputation wouldn't be besmirched. He refused, of course, and so his mother and brother put into play the rumors, the slander that forced his hand.

To this day, that decision haunted him, and now, standing before Molly, he knew his truth would be the end of their newly forming friendship.

She would hate him for the fiend, the lying ass that he was. The bastard he'd been.

And so this morning, he had fled Rome. Had ridden out before dawn, determined to leave Molly and the temptation she brought to his life. The wants and needs to be a man she could love, admire, and marry. He had started toward Naples, removing himself from her life, leaving her to her holiday and tours, not being a distraction in her world.

He may be the Duke of St. Albans now, but his brother had gone to his grave, the respectable, noble god. Hugh was the degenerate, scandalous sibling who ruined innocent women and broke families apart.

True or not, it was what everyone believed.

"I want you. With each breath that I breathe, I want you more, and yet I cannot have you." With each inhalation, her towel lifted, giving him a small glimpse of her ample bosom. Her skin was fragrant, smelled of sweet flowers, and his mouth watered with the want that thrummed through him. He wanted to kiss, taste his way over her skin, gorge on her until he was satisfied.

Which, he was starting to believe, would never be the case.

Her tongue came out, licking her lips at his words, and his cock hardened. He was acting as bad as his brother, wanting to deflower an innocent woman just to quell his wicked appetites.

"Why can we not be together? If we both choose to be so?" Molly asked him, her eyes, fathomless pools of need he could happily drown in as she stared at him, waited for him to answer.

The answer was as complicated as his emotions toward the woman standing before him. Tangled and caught up about them. If she only knew the truth, the answer to her question would be simple. He would never even have the opportunity to court her, for she would never have given him a second glance. "You're a virgin, an unmarried maid. I will not ruin you," he said instead.

"I'm also eight and twenty. I think I am old enough to choose my path. To determine what I want and when I want it. I want you too, Hugh." She sighed, stepping closer to him, the linen of her towel teasing his chest. "I do not understand what is happening to me, but when I'm around you, all I can think about is your touch. I ache in places for you that I did not know existed before we met. I—"

He kissed her. Hard. Took her mouth in a searing kiss that startled him in its intensity. To stand there, hearing her words, was torture he could not endure. Her tongue tangled with his, her arms wrapping about his neck, her towel forgotten.

He reached behind her, pulling it free from her body. His hands snaked across her skin and clasped her ass, picking her up to straddle him. She gasped against his lips, but did not shy away, kissed him with an abandon that left him reeling for purpose.

A voice, a drum in his mind told him to stop. That this was wrong, he was acting like his brother, but he could not.

He could no sooner deny her needs than he could deny himself air.

This is not what he'd thought would occur between them when he'd first met her, but having grown to know her over the past week, he realized that it was inevitable they would come together. The attraction, the sizzling air that always circulated about them when they were together, was proof enough that they would become one.

She undulated against his cock, moaning through their kiss, and he walked them over to the bath. He set her down, ripping his shirt over his head and throwing it away somewhere over his back. The touch of her hands on the buttons of his breeches made his stomach quake. She made short work of them, ripping his pants open and assisting him in pulling them down. She stood back, staring at him, a wicked glint and admiration in her eyes as she took her fill.

Hugh stood before her, quiet and willing for her to enjoy what was hers. For it was true. He was hers, forever after this night. He would never look at another woman, not after bedding such a sweet, beautiful being such as his Molly.

Molly took his hand, leading him into the water. The bath was hot, the fragrant scent of flowers permeating from the steam. Hugh stood to the side of the bath, leaning up against it as he watched her float about in the water before him. Hell, she was beautiful, made his heart ache.

"You're too far away." The words reverberated about in his mind, forcing him to take into account that she only had three weeks left with him before leaving for England. He could not let her go. To remain in Rome without her left a hollow, gaping wound deep in his chest.

He'd been content before, went about his days busy with his estates, with his winery in Naples, but to think of going back to the way his life was before Molly was no longer possible. He already knew he would pine for her, miss her, want her until it drove him mad, or pushed him back to England. A country that he would not return to, not after it turned against him without a second thought.

Her lips twisted into a teasing grin, and she swam up against him, straddling him. The breath in his lungs seized at the slippery, willing feel of her in his arms. He tamped down his rakish needs that wanted to seize, conquer, and take what she was so obviously willing to give.

He kissed her, starved of her since the last they were together. He could get used to having her just as they were. Alone and as if the world and its prejudices could not touch them, would not impinge on their decisions or life.

"Stay with me in Rome," he pleaded, holding her fast against him, biting back a groan when her naked self slipped against his cock.

"I will be honest with you, Hugh, because I don't want any secrets between us, but I cannot stay. Not because I do not want to, but because I will not be your mistress. I will not be anyone's mistress."

He frowned, tipping up her chin so she would look at him. "I do not want you to be my mistress. I want more from you than that." He wanted her to be his wife, but how could he ask her to be so when she didn't know anything about him, and when she did, she would likely scorn and run for the hills.

It was a risk he would have to take, for damn it all to hell, he didn't want to lose the woman in his arms. She was perfect for him in every way. For the first time in his life, he was where he wanted to be and with the woman who completed his circle of happiness.

"How much more?" she asked him, her eyes full of trepidation at what his next words would be.

"I know we have not known each other for long, hell, we hardly know each other, but for the first time in my existence, I know what I feel is right. It is what I want and what I want most of all is you. Will you marry me, Molly? Be mine?"

*M*olly stared at Hugh, her mind a kaleidoscope of thoughts over why she should not marry him. Why the answer to this question ought to be a no, they did not know each other, had met but a week before. Even so, the thought of saying no to the man who held her in his arms and watched her with something akin to fear lurking in the deep depths of his eyes, was impossible to fathom. She wanted to marry him, to be his and no one else's.

She also knew that never had she felt about anyone else how she felt about Hugh. Her body came alive when he was around. Today when she had explored the markets alone and without Hugh, only Miss Sinclair for company, she realized that a little spark that lit Rome to a glowing beacon was not there. Hugh made her travels about the city enjoyable, brought humor and knowledge, gave her a taste of this foreign, ancient city she would otherwise not have experienced.

She was falling in love with him as much as her mind had fallen in love with Rome.

Molly stared at him, so very thankful that she had found the man before her. A man who would be hers forever. All hers and no one else's, even if she had to travel halfway around the world to find him. "Yes. Yes, I will marry you."

He smiled before kissing her. His mouth was hot, insistent, and her body hummed for completion, to be taken and inflamed. Her skin was on fire, and she could not help but rub against him, seek the pleasure that she knew he could give her.

Hugh spun them about, pushing her up against the side of the bath. He hoisted her higher on his hip, his cock teasing her core. She groaned, laying her head against the bath's tiled side as he worked her aching flesh to an inferno. "Yes, take me. I want you so much." Molly didn't care she was begging, or that he had so much power over her at present. All she cared about was that he would make love to her. Give her what she wanted and had not known she'd been missing all these years.

"I can wait, Molly. We do not have to do this now. We can be married within a few days and then come together if you would prefer."

"No." She shook her head, not wanting to wait that long. A time that seemed as far away as the moon. "I want you now. Please, give me what I want." *You*. She didn't say the word, but her mind chanted it like a drum.

His clasp on her bottom tightened, and then she felt him, the hard, silky-smooth head of his manhood pressing against her core. He watched her as slowly, inch by delicious inch, he filled her. With the water's help and her need for him, Molly did not feel the stinging pain she expected. Surprisingly she did not feel anything but exquisite pleasure.

Molly reached up, clasping Hugh's jaw and bringing him to her for a kiss. She gasped as he thrust the last inch of himself into her. Her body urged him to move, and then he did. He thrust into her, joining them forever, and Molly knew what it was to feel loved.

His pumps were deep and constant. Each one hitting a special little place deep in her core. Need ran through her, hot and wild. She held on to him, pushing against him, taking everything he was giving. Her whole center shifted to where they joined, the need to reach whatever apex he was forcing her toward.

"Fuck, you make me burn." His hot breath rasped against her neck. He nipped her skin before laving the bite with his tongue. A shiver rocked through her, and she sighed. "So tight. Mine."

"So big," she retorted. He groaned, the sound a mixture of pleasure and pain. His hand closed over her breast, his thumb and forefinger pinching her nipple. A shot of awareness raced through her body, heightening her pleasure.

"Come for me, my darling."

His words whispered against her ear were her undoing. A feeling unlike one she'd ever experienced ricocheted from her sex and out to every part of her body. A delicious tremor of pleasure convulsed from her sex to the tips of her fingers. Molly screamed his name, but Hugh did not stop. His thrusts only heightened her pleasure, sending waves to convulse through her blood.

"Hugh," she gasped, letting him take her, fuck her as he said and stoke the fire he had ignited in her soul.

"Molly," he groaned, as he too found release, his seed rushing into her core as he followed her climax with his. Their breathing ragged, they stood locked together. She clasped him tight, holding him against her as she tried to calm her racing heart. Molly had never felt so satisfied in her life, so fulfilled and inflamed.

"When can we marry?" she asked, kissing him as he regained his breath.

He grinned, chuckling at her question. "Is tomorrow too soon?"

She grinned back. "Tomorrow sounds perfect."

CHAPTER 9

Tomorrow wasn't too soon. Molly stood beside Hugh in a quaint, Roman church just outside the city and took her vows to be his wife. Miss Sinclair and Marcus stood as their witnesses.

Molly glanced up at Hugh, not believing that she would soon be his wife. A partner to a man who had made a successful life for himself away from England. Her husband. Which would mean Rome would be her home from this day forward. She did not care that he was not titled, or that her marrying him may limit her time with her friends back in England. They would be happy for her because she had found the man she loved.

A man who loved her in return.

Heat rushed onto her cheeks at the thought of their wedding night. Tonight, they could sleep together in the villa. Not apart like they had to when they had returned from the bathhouse only a day before.

To imagine that time was only yesterday was beyond comprehension. It a matter of only a few hours they were uniting their two families. Had her skin not been holding her together, she was sure she would burst apart with excitement.

"I now pronounce you husband and wife," the priest declared, smiling down at them.

Hugh turned to her, the love shining back in his eyes, humbling her. He took her hand and kissed her gloved fingers, his intense, burning stare watching her as he bestowed the sweet gesture.

She wore a ballgown that she had made for last year's Season, a blue so light in the shade that at times it could almost appear white. Molly glanced at her new husband. The idea that she had traveled partway around the world and met a gentleman who made her body and mind not her own, and marry him was an idea so foreign to her she couldn't believe it was real. She'd never acted so rashly and made a decision that would affect the rest of her life so quickly.

Marcus and Miss Sinclair clapped at the celebration of their union, coming up to them before they signed the paperwork to officiate their day.

"Are you happy, my darling wife?" Hugh asked her as he helped her into his carriage, shutting the door behind them and enclosing them in a space all for themselves, away from servants and her companion.

"I'm so happy and a little dazed. I've never made such a huge decision like this before in my life and so quickly."

"You do not regret it, I hope." A shadow of fear lurked in his eyes, and Molly closed the space between them, coming to sit on his lap. She wrapped her arms about his neck, holding him close.

"I will never regret marrying you. I adore you. I hope you know that."

"I love you so very much, Molly."

His declaration sat between them, a knot that tied her to him forever, for she had fallen headlong and absolutely in love with the man in her arms. He was her equal, the man who made her a better person. He filled her life with adventure and laughter. She snuck a quick kiss, running her hands through his hair and pushing it away from his face so she could see his gorgeous visage better.

"I love you too. You're a gift that Rome has bestowed on me that I had not thought to receive."

His hands wrenched her higher on his lap, her bottom snug between his legs. He kissed her. Hard. Molly threw herself into the kiss, showing him how much she cared and loved the man in her arms.

His tongue tangled with hers, sending a bolt of desire to her core. She ached for him, longed for his touch the moment they had parted ways the night before after their delightful bath together.

Now she never had to leave his side if she did not choose to. She could kiss and touch, play, and have him whenever she wanted. The idea was an elixir that she could get used to, and quickly, she mused.

His tongue tangled with hers, his hands slipping up her waist to clasp her breast. He wrenched the bodice down. Cool air kissed her breast before his hot, warm mouth brushed her skin. His lips worked her flesh, his tongue flicking out to tease her nipple. It beaded, and on a sigh, she closed her eyes, reveling in his touch.

"I want you. I cannot wait."

"Me, either." He lifted her off his lap, a feat had he not done it she would've thought impossible. She was a tall woman and with womanly curves, and yet, he lifted her as if she weighed no more than a piece of parchment.

Molly only stood before him a moment before he had

her straddle his hips. His hands fumbled with her gown, dragging it up to pool about her waist. Her wet core met with his hardened manhood, and she understood what he was about. Expectation thrummed through her veins. He reached between them, flicked his front falls open with little finesse. She shivered, need riding her hard, and then he was there. Pushing into her wet heat, his thick, firm manhood filling her to completion.

The carriage rolled through the streets, the sounds and smells of Rome but a passing thought as he took her, hard and fast in their enclosed sanctuary. Molly held on to him for purpose, riding him as he instructed. The position gave her power over him she liked, a heady experience that Hugh seemed to savor as well.

She kissed him, lifting herself and using the carriage's rocking movement to her advantage.

"Yes, fuck me. God damn it, you're beautiful and mine. All mine."

"Yes," she gasped as the first tremors of pleasure started to thrum through her body. Molly wanted more of the same, greedy for the pleasure he could launch into her life. She slammed down on him, took her pleasure, rode his manhood, and pushed herself into the abyss of ecstasy.

Hugh kissed her scream into submission as their mouths and bodies fused. His own moan tangled with hers.

She slumped against him, half on his lap and the cushioned seat. "I do not think I shall ever view a carriage ride the same."

He grinned down at her, a small flush spreading across his cheeks and making him look like a green lad who'd just been extremely naughty with a woman. "I aim to please and show you all the magnificent heights of this city that you can have."

Molly chuckled, laying her head on his shoulder and looking out the window. "We did not even close the blinds. I hope no one was watching our carriage too closely."

He shrugged, one hand idly rubbing her arm just below her sleeve. "Let them talk should they have seen us. I was making love with my wife. There is no sin in that."

No, she mused. There was not.

~

*H*ugh was the veriest bastard under the sun, but he would repair his sin. He would make things right with Molly when he told her the truth. He just needed time. Now that she was not returning to England, he would explain to her the truth of his past, why he was in Rome, and face her wrath then.

When she could not run away from him. Not without a fight.

With Molly's humble family, it was a possibility that she'd never even heard of his family, of what he was charged with having done. His brother had not married, had merely carried on his wayward ways, except Hugh supposed he did learn a valuable lesson in not dallying with unmarried maids and kept his bed partners to widows or married women.

He was thankful that not all his friends had thought him a cad, had not believed the slur on his name. The Duke of Whitstone one of them. His Grace had been at his estate when his brother's missive had descended on him, demanding he take the fall.

Had Whitstone not been visiting his home when his brother's note arrived, his good friend too may have not have believed him. Hugh was far from a saint and had had his fair share of lovers, although he'd never dallied with virginal debutantes.

Stupid Henry had ruined so many things the day he wet his cock in a cunny that he should never have touched.

Molly, too was friends with Whitstone and trusted the duke. If he wrote to his friend, had him help him explain that was he was accused of was incorrect, there may be no impediment to their marriage working.

He could not lose her now. He loved her with an intensity that scared him and one he'd not thought to ever experience.

Hugh helped her alight from the carriage. He leaned down, picking her up before carrying her over the threshold of their villa, their home, and where he hoped they would start a family. Thanking the staff who lined up to congratulate them, they hastily made their way upstairs toward his suite of rooms. Their room from this night onward. He slammed the door closed, turning the lock and shutting the world away from their sanctuary.

Molly made short work of her gown, throwing her veil to the side and stepping out of her silk slippers as she watched him. Her luscious hair fell about her shoulders, her eyes glinting with expectation.

Hugh ripped his cravat free. His coat and waistcoat soon followed along with his breeches. "Get on the bed," he ordered, striding over to her with a casual air that was the opposite to how he felt.

Inside, his body quivered with need. Already he wanted her again. To lose himself in her hot, tight cunny. To make love to the woman who was a gift he'd not thought to ever receive.

"What are you going to do to me?" She did as he bade, sitting on the bed before scuttling back a little on the linen.

Hugh came to stand before her. He dropped to his knees. Her eyes widened, and she let out a little squeal when he clasped her ankles and pulled her to the edge of the mattress.

"Lay back," he ordered. Without question, she did as he asked, her breathing ragged. He took in her beauty, her small stomach he hoped would bloom and stretch with their children in years to come. He pushed her legs apart, giving him a view of her cunny. She glistened in the afternoon light, and the musky, sweet scent of her teased his senses.

His mouth watered with the thought of tasting her, eating her until he was sated. His cock twitched, jutting out in front of him, primed and ready. He stoked it quickly, teasing himself. He wanted to come, to fuck her, but that could wait. Right now, he wanted to make her shatter on his lips. To hear her scream his name and grind herself against his face like he'd dreamed about this past week.

He cast a quick look up at Molly and found her watching him, her perfect, white teeth clamping her bottom lip in expectation. Hugh reached up, sliding his hand across her stomach to squeeze her breast. "You're going to love this, my love."

Hugh leaned forward, kissing his way up her leg, taking little love bites as he went. She squirmed under his assault, and he grinned, knowing there would be a lot more squirming by the end of the night.

He licked her skin, it smelled of spring flowers. Hell, she was sweet, so willing and reactive. He was a lucky man to have married such a woman. He licked his lips, rubbing his thumb over her nubbin, coating his finger in her juices. She moaned but didn't shy away from his touch, instead, she spread her legs wider, her wicked gaze begging him to do more.

Oh, he'd do more, so much more before they had finished their first night as a married couple. Unable to wait a moment longer, he slid his tongue along her cunny. He used slow, smooth strokes, the need to savor the taste of her on his lips stopping him from rushing. Her fingers clamped into his hair, holding him at her core, and he ate her sweet petal, licking and flicking her receptive nubbin until she was writhing with need.

He had imagined Molly just so, letting him bring her to climax. Hugh placed his hands beneath her bottom, pulling her closer to his mouth and kissed her there. Used his tongue to tease, to delve. With one finger, he slipped into her. Her body clamped down on him, and his cock twitched, beaded with his own seed.

So tight. So hot.

Patience, he reminded himself. This right now was all for his wife. To give her pleasure without having to receive any in return. Not physically, in any case. In truth, however, his cock stood erect, poised for release. To give pleasure was just as exciting as receiving in his estimation.

She rode him, lost all inhibitions, and let him love her. His mouth made love to her, his finger teasing and giving a glimpse of what was to come. His cock.

"Oh, Hugh. Yes. Ohhh," she said, her thrusts frenzied. *Almost there.* He grinned, flicking her nubbin one last time. She broke apart before him, arms outstretched above her head, her body riding his face without thought or care.

She was fucking marvelous.

CHAPTER 10

*T*he day after their wedding, Hugh surprised Molly with a trip to his villa in Naples. The carriage journey took several days, but upon arriving at his villa, which overlooked the Bay of Naples, she realized the jarring of her bones and numbness of her bottom was well worth the discomfort.

Behind the villa were fields of grapevines, ideal growing in the rich volcanic soil. They were abundant and the deepest green she'd ever beheld, and already an abundance of grapes hung heavy on the vine.

Molly stood out the front of the villa on her first night, Naples lights tinkling in the early evening, the sunset a rich red and orange. Still visible in the distance was the majestic Mt. Vesuvius.

Hugh came up behind her, wrapping his arms about her waist. "Do you wish to see Pompei and Herculaneum? We can travel down there in a day or two if it pleases you."

Molly clasped his arms, holding him to her. It was surreal that she was here, married, and in love. So much had happened to her in such a short period of time that if her feet were not firmly on the ground, she might swoon.

"You're spoiling me. My friend Hallie will be terribly jealous when I tell her of all the places that I've been to."

"She enjoys travel as much as you?" His words tickled her ear, and she shivered in the warm, evening air.

"She lived in Egypt for some years. She's a historian, but is now married to the Viscount Duncannon."

"Arthur?" Hugh said.

Molly turned to him, meeting his gaze. "Do you know Lord Duncannon too? I did not know that you knew many other people in the *ton* other than the Duke of Whitstone."

"I, um, know a little of him, yes. Through Whitstone."

Molly wondered at his words before he pulled her into the room just off the balcony where his housekeeper here had served up cold meats, bread, and pasta for dinner. Molly sat and smiled as Hugh didn't move to the end of the table, but sat beside her, reaching out to pick up her hand and kiss it.

"I'm so very fortunate to have you as my wife. I want to spoil you most definitely, so tell me what you would like to do tomorrow. We may go and see if the gardeners at the Royal Palace of Caserta will allow us to walk the grounds. The building is as majestic as Versailles."

"Truly?" Molly had never heard of such a place, but having seen and adored Versailles, another such building of similar architectural beauty would be an excellent location to visit. "I would love that. May we also visit the sea? They say the water is aqua in color, and I want to know if that is true."

Hugh chuckled, placing a large portion of chicken and ham onto his plate, along with a good helping of pasta. "Your wish is my command, my love. Do you wish to go sea bathing? I can arrange that for you as well if you like."

Excitement thrummed through her veins, and Molly knew she was grinning like a spoiled child getting everything that she wished. "Will you join me if I do?"

The heated look he threw her sent her blood to pump hard in her veins, and she clasped her stomach to stop its fluttering. "Do you need ask?"

Molly bit her lip, spooning a mouthful of pasta into her mouth. "No, but I wanted to make certain just in case."

Their days in Naples were full of laughter and pleasure. Simply the two of them, exploring, learning, and always loving when they came together at night.

Pompeii and Herculaneum took some days to visit. Walking about the areas of Pompeii, especially, left Molly with a sense of the gravity of what had happened to the people there. The excavation of the buried city was in its infancy, from looking at what had been unearthed so far, so much more of the ancient city remained hidden.

They had walked the beach in the Bay of Naples, and sea bathed just as Hugh had promised. The weeks sped by, and before she knew it, they had been in Naples a month.

They returned to Rome tomorrow, and Molly had to admit she did not want to leave. This city, its beauty, the mountains, and fields full of fertile, rich crops had imbedded into her heart, much like the man sitting at his desk right at this moment.

Molly put down the knitting she had started while here and stood, walking over to his desk. She ran her hands over his shoulders, sliding them down over his arms and peeking at the many letters that sat scattered before him.

He leaned back in his chair, smiling up at her. "What are you up to, my darling wife?"

She chuckled, coming about and sitting herself down on his lap. He adjusted her, hugging her to him before kissing her soundly. Molly melted into his arms, knowing when they returned to Rome, she would count down the days until they were back here again, alone and in their own little cocoon.

She ran her hands through his hair, putting it on end. "Thank you for this wonderful holiday. I feel so very blessed to have found you."

"No, it is I who has been honored. I feel I shall never be able to pay Whitstone back for the tremendous deed he's done by sending you to me."

Molly chuckled. "I'm certain he could think of something. Probably involve buying a thoroughbred if I'm to guess correctly."

Hugh nodded, his gaze darkening with desire. "No doubt."

*H*ugh lifted Molly to sit on his desk. Her delectable rump in his lap drove him to distraction, and for the past hour of working on paperwork from his estate here in Naples, he'd not been able to concentrate.

The sight of his wife, biting her lip, and attempting to knit, which did not seem to be a skill she was very adept at had warmed his blood. When she'd finally come over to see what he was about, he knew he would not let her go again.

Papers scattered to the floor. He slid his hand along her leg, liking that his wife had disregarded her use of stockings in the Italian heat. Her soft skin tempted him like no other, and he squeezed her thigh, electing a sigh from her delectable lips.

He could not wait a moment longer, and kissed her, pulled her to the edge of the desk and stepped between her legs. She opened for him, lifting her leg to rest about his waist.

Hugh fumbled for his front falls, ripping them open and freeing his hard cock, and then he was in her. They gasped at the contact, each time they came together was like the first. Hugh wondered if it would always be like this with Molly—all-consuming and wild, as hot as the midday sun.

She moaned, laying back on the desk, and she was his to have. Seeing her before him, his for the taking, her breasts rocking with each thrust caused his balls to tighten, his cock to swell.

He ran his hand up her hip to her breast, squeezing the ample flesh just as she liked. Hugh leaned over her, thrusting deeper, harder, and he knew she was close.

She mewled beneath him, without fear or reserve. She sighed his name, her hands reaching behind her for the desk's edge for purchase.

Hugh brought his hand down to her cunny, wet and tight. He slid his thumb over her engorged nubbin, and she came apart beneath him. Her core convulsing and pulling his own release forward.

Hugh fucked her hard, let himself go over the edge before slumping beside her on his desk, heedless of the mess their lovemaking had caused.

Her chest rose and fell rapidly with exertion, and he laughed, feeling his own heart beat hard and loud in his chest.

"I do not think I shall ever get tired of such an activity. You've positively ruined me forever."

He sighed, pulling her into the crook of his arm. "I adore you too," he said, kissing her temple. "Shall we adjourn to the bathhouse? I know how much you love to bathe."

She grinned, her cheeks a light-pink shade that made his heart miss a beat. "You know me so well, husband. Let us go."

~

A week later, Molly woke in their bedroom in Rome, so very thankful that the world was a different place to where it was only a month before. She was a wife. Mrs Molly Armstrong. The thought could not make her happier.

She sighed, rolling over and smiling at the curtains that billowed in the morning breeze. Hugh was not beside her, but then he often was not in the morning. An early riser her husband seemed to be, and was the opposite of who Molly had always been. But then, her seeking him out in his office had become a bit of a game, and a most pleasurable one each day.

A knock sounded on her door, and she bade enter her new lady's maid, a young Italian woman who was the housekeeper's granddaughter. The young woman had wanted to rise above being a maid in the household and had come to Molly, asking if she may practice as her maid.

She had agreed straightaway, and Miss Sinclair seemed only too happy to go back to her ways of watching from afar, and reading each day and not having to be so very busy trying to keep a watch on Molly. Now that she was a wife, Miss Sinclair had agreed to stay for a few more weeks and then travel back to London. Although from the growing affection between her companion and Marcus, something told Molly that a second wedding may soon occur.

Cassia bobbed a quick curtsy, before holding up two gowns neatly pressed. "Good morning, *Signora* Molly. What dress would you prefer for the ball this evening?"

Ah yes, the Earl and Countess Brandon's ball that she had been invited to. Hugh had been less pleased for Molly to attend, and it was odd that the invitation had only been addressed to her. Perhaps Lady Brandon had not heard of her marriage and still assumed she was visiting Rome alone with her companion.

"The red silk is very pretty. I shall wear that tonight."

"You shall look beautiful in the dress," Hugh's deep baritone said from the doorway. He leaned against the stone, a contemplative look on his handsome visage.

Butterflies took flight in Molly's stomach, and she jumped from the bed, dismissing her maid who scurried from the room. She pulled Hugh toward a seat that sat before their unlit hearth. "Sit," she ordered him. His eyes widened in question before he did as she bade.

"What are you doing?" he asked, a mischievous glint in his orbs.

Molly kneeled before him, running her hands along the top of his thighs, the buckskin breeches under her palms soft to touch, and yet the muscle beneath bunched and pulled tight.

"If I'm to look fetching in my gown, it is only because I've married the most handsome man in Italy, and he's my escort."

"About that," he said, running a hand over his jaw. "I

cannot attend the ball this evening. Some estate business has arrived from England that I need to go over. I'm very sorry, my love. Will you forgive me?" He leaned forward, kissing her. His lips were soft, warm, and desire thrummed in her veins.

Would it always be like this for her with Hugh? Would she always crave him as much as she wanted him at this very moment?

"I can attend on my own. I'm sure I shall endure the ball very well without you, but I shall miss you." She smiled, wanting to put him at ease. "I am, after all, quite used to attending such events by myself."

Hugh frowned, reaching for her. "I do not want you to go on your own. Why not stay here with me and we shall attend to our own festivity? Just the two of us?"

Molly chuckled, a wicked idea coming to mind. She reached up to the clasps on his breeches, meeting Hugh's gaze as her fingers made light work of the buttons. A sinful glint entered Hugh's eyes, and he adjusted his seat to help assist her in pulling his breeches down.

His manhood sprung free, fully erect and all hers. This close and in the daylight, she could study him much better, play, and learn. Molly ran a finger along a large vein that ran from the base of his penis to the head. A small droplet of moisture beaded on the top, and she ran her finger over it, rubbing it between her thumb and forefinger. It was smooth, just like his manhood itself. Never before had anything felt so soft. A velvety skin over hard steel. An amazing thing really when one thought about it, and she was both fascinated and tempted to learn more about what she could do with it now that it was hers to savor.

Molly leaned forward and licked the tip of his penis. It

was salty, dissimilar to anything she'd sampled before, but not disagreeable. Hugh's hands clamped the sides of his chair, grounding himself still. Molly cast him a swift look. His jaw clenched, a small muscle pulsated at his temple. Even so he did not attempt to stop her, or guide her in her journey.

She leaned forward, this time licking the full length of him, from base to tip. His intake of breath spurred her on, and she suckled the tip of his manhood before taking him fully in her mouth. Her tongue rasped against his member, and Hugh pumped his hips, guiding her with his hands tangled in her hair how he liked it.

Molly liked it too. Loved that she could tease him, love him in this way just as he'd similarly loved her. She had fallen quite in love with Hugh's kisses against her cunny and had wondered if it were possible for her to give the same pleasure in return.

It would seem that it was so.

"Yes, suck me like that," he gasped, pushing deep into her mouth. Molly reveled in the feel of his manhood in her mouth, hard and deep. She reached down, touching herself, aching for him to do the same, anything that would sate her need of him.

"Oh, no, you do not," he said, pulling her off him.

Before Molly knew what he was about, he'd stood, pushing her to lean against the chair he vacated. Cool morning air kissed the backs of her legs, and she glanced over her shoulder to see her shift lifted to reveal her bottom.

Molly held on to the chair, expectation thrumming through her as Hugh positioned himself behind, and then he filled her. Thrust into her aching self and took her, hard and fast. Molly muffled her moans in the chair's cushion.

Hugh took her rough and hard, everything that she wanted.

"Oh, yes. Hugh," she moaned. He reached about her waist and teased her flesh, rubbing her with his fingers and taunting her until she did not know where she began, and he ended. It was too much. The pleasure, the need too strong. He would break her into a million pieces and she would never go back together again. She mumbled incoherently as he took her, his hard chest coming over her back, holding her close as thrust after thrust pumped into her core.

And she was lost.

*H*ugh fucked Molly with a need that scared him. He could not get enough of his new wife, not just in this way but also in every way. To be near her was to be content, happy. He'd not felt that for a very long time.

He held her as he pumped into her tight, wet heat. Damn it, she was perfect, reactive, and always surprising him with her needs and desires. He'd not come to her room this morning to receive such a gift, and he would not leave until she too had pleasure.

The scent of flowers wafted from her hair. He breathed deep, knowing he would never get enough of her. She pushed back on him, taking her pleasure as much as he was giving, and he felt the tightening, the convulsing of her core about his cock. She screamed his name into the cushions. Hugh fucked her, let himself be pulled into climax by her spasming heat. He came hard, spilled his seed deep, and reveled in the satisfaction that came over him at having Molly in his life.

Hell, he loved her. So much.

Hugh disengaged, and pulling her shift down, picked her up and carried her to their bed. Not the easiest feat as he'd only removed his breeches from one leg in his haste to have her. He kicked off his pants and climbed into bed next to her, pulling her into the crook of his arm.

"Are you happy?" He needed to know that she was. That their time together was nothing but a happy one for Molly. She was the most important person in his world now, and he would do everything to protect and love her as much as she deserved.

"I'm so happy." She grinned up at him, snuggling down against his side, one arm thrown lazily over his stomach.

Hugh closed his eyes and yawned, tired and satisfied.

"Are you certain you cannot come to the ball with me tonight? I want to show off my new husband."

Hugh would love to go, but he could not. Lord Brandon was recently in Rome from London, and he knew of his past. The accusations, no matter how false, would be revealed if he attended. Even using his mother's maiden name of Armstrong, Lord Brandon knew his face. Would out him to Molly.

He needed to tell her the truth himself, just not yet. He wasn't ready for that conversation right now.

If he could, he'd persuade Molly to stay home with him, enjoy more of their time together, such as they just did.

"You could always not go and stay at home with me, as I suggested before."

"But you said you had work to do. I would only be in your way, and in any case, I'm looking forward to seeing Lady Brandon. She will have news from home, and as much as I love being here with you, I do miss my friends."

Hugh pushed back a lock of hair from Molly's face, marveling at her beauty. "I know you do, my love. You should go and enjoy yourself." He paused, pulling the bedding up over them more. "And I promise you the next ball that is to take place in Rome, I shall attend."

She turned and kissed his chest, and a bolt of pleasure thrummed through his blood. His cocked twitched, ready and willing to go again. Having a wife had made him the most rakish being in Christendom.

"Very well. I'm satisfied with those terms. I hope you shall miss me tonight?"

Hugh rolled Molly onto her back, settling between her legs. His cock hard and primed to go again. Her eyes darkened with need, and she wiggled, placing him at her core. Desire licked at the base of his spine, and he pushed into her a little way, teasing them both.

"Oh, I shall miss you, and when you return home, you will know how much."

"Mmmm," she gasped, lifting her legs about his back and pulling him into her.

Hugh bit back a groan. His wife was a hellion, and he loved every moment of it. "Are you after something, wife?" he teased, holding her and his need at bay.

She pouted, squirming on him and making him see stars. "You know I am." Her words were breathless, an edge of annoyance to her tone. Hugh chuckled.

"Tell me what you want." He needed to hear it from her. Hear her ask for him.

"You," she gasped. "I want you."

Hugh thrust into her, pleasure rocked through him, strong and hard, and he was lost. Lost in the arms of his wife. A place that he never wanted to venture from. Not today, or ever.

CHAPTER 11

$\mathcal{T}$he ball at Lord and Lady Brandon's was a crush. Molly arrived a little late after her husband came to their room to wish her a good evening, and they had ended up toppled onto the bed, enjoying each other instead.

Molly came into the atrium of the villa, the introductions long past, and made her way over to her hosts for the evening. She dipped into a curtsy. Lady Brandon beamed at her arrival, pulling her into a quick embrace. "Molly, my dear. How wonderful to find you in Rome. When Ava said you had traveled here, I was so pleased. We must have you over for lunch when you're free."

"I would like that very much." Lady Brandon took Molly's arm, turning her away from the party.

"Let us take a turn about the room. I feel there is so much to discuss. How has your holiday been so far? I understand you were to only stay a month, but you just returned from Naples, no? Has something changed in your circumstances to keep you here in my incredible home country?"

Molly wondered if she should tell her friend of her marriage. She had not written to her family as yet and would hate for the news of her nuptials to reach them from someone else other than herself. She would ensure that tonight she would write the necessary letters. "I was to return and join the Duchess of Whitstone, and Countess Duncannon in London for the new Season. That, however, will no longer occur. I'm going to be staying in Rome for some time."

"Why is that? Do you like the city so very much that you have decided to make it your permanent address?"

Molly nodded, unable to hold back the smile at the thought of Hugh in her life.

"I was married last month, my lady. It has been a whirl-wind courtship, but one that I do not regret. I have found the man of my heart, and I shall make Rome my home since this is his home also."

"Oh, my darling friend, I cannot believe it." Lady Brandon blushed a little, before taking two glasses of champagne from a passing servant. "Not that I do not believe that anyone should not wish to marry you, but that you have accepted him. I always thought you were settled as a spinster—a woman who enjoyed her independence. A point proven I believe by the fact that you're in Rome and only with a companion for company. How is Miss Sinclair? Still complaining about doing what she is paid to do?"

Molly chuckled, sipping her fruity drink. "Not at all. I do believe my companion has fallen for a handsome servant of my husband. I think it is only a matter of time before they marry. I do not see her returning to England anytime soon."

"Well, that is delightful news." Her ladyship beamed at her, her eyes bright and eager for news. "Tell me of the gentleman who has won your heart? Is he someone we would know? Is he a Roman man? We all know how very lovely they can be," she said with a wink. "It would not surprise me that one has captured your heart, my dear."

All true, of course, but not in this case. "He's English, has lived abroad for several years now. Mr. Hugh Armstrong is his name. Have you heard of him?"

Lady Brandon pulled back a little, the color draining from her cheeks.

Molly reached out to her, taking her arm. "Are you well, Rose? You've become quite pale."

Her ladyship shook herself a little before continuing. "Do you mean to tell me that Lord Hugh Armstrong, Lord Farley when he left England and is now the Duke of St. Albans, is your husband?"

The name Farley bounced about in her mind. Molly shook her head, clearing it of the troublesome thought that she'd married a man who went by the same name as the gentleman who had ruined her cousin's life.

"Pardon?" she said, unable to voice more words. There were hundreds of Farleys, and in Italy, surely. A common name that wasn't always linked with nobility. That Lady Brandon had jumped to the conclusion Hugh was the man who had ruined all her cousin's hopes and dreams, had left her heartbroken before she died was unfathomable.

It could not be Hugh.

"I do not think Mr. Armstrong is who you mean. I thought Lord Farley had traveled to Spain, not Rome."

Lady Brandon glanced about them, checking that they were alone. "I may be mistaken, but did I not hear a rumor that your family has a distant association with the St. Albans? Your cousin, Miss Cox, was ruined by Lord Farley. Is that not correct?"

Molly frowned, panic clawing at her chest. "How do you know that? No one knows of the connection. My family was very careful to keep others from being tainted by Laura's social demise."

"Ah, well as to that. When I married Lord Brandon and returned to England with him from Italy, I hired a dressmaker. She happened to be the late Miss Cox's dressmaker, and I heard a time or two little tidbits of information. Your name was said along with Miss Cox's, and it wasn't hard to assume a blood connection. You do look very similar to Miss Cox. I was aware of her during her first Season."

Molly nodded, swallowing as bile rose in her throat. If Lady Brandon knew of Laura and her connection to Molly, how many other people in London did also? Was that why she had never had any offers to her hand? Did they think her, too, fallen from grace?

Heat rushed to her face, and she took a fortifying sip of her wine. Hugh could not be Lord Farley. And what was this about him being a duke?

"You mentioned Lord Farley is now the Duke St. Albans. What has happened to his older brother?"

Her ladyship pursed her lips, a displeased line to her mouth. "Racing his curricle and lost control of the vehicle. Killed both himself and his valet. Before we caught our ship to Rome, it was all London was talking of."

Lord Farley could not be her husband. He could not. She would not believe such a thing. "Mr. Armstrong is not whom you speak of. I'm certain of it."

"Armstrong was the surname of the late Duchess St. Albans. It was her maiden name. I think I'm correct in this, Molly. I think this is too much of a coincidence to be an error."

Molly glanced about the room. She breathed deep, needing air. Her gown was too tight, her skin too heated. The room spun, and she clasped her ladyship for purchase. "May we go someplace else? I cannot think straight in this room."

"Of course," Lady Brandon bustled her out of the atrium and into a nearby sitting room that was thankfully empty. "Mr. Armstrong, your husband, is who I believe him to be, is he not?"

This could not be true. Hugh could not be the one and the same man whom she'd sworn to hate for all eternity. "I cannot believe it. It cannot be so."

"But I think it is so, my dear. Miss Laura Cox was your cousin, was she not? I'm not wrong in that."

"You are not wrong." Her answer came out but a whisper, and she could not believe the words. The life that she had hoped to live evaporated before her eyes. A little mocking voice taunted her that this is what happened when one married without knowing the other person for very long. That this was a sign that she was not meant for love or marriage. That she should have been content being alone and having herself for company.

"Whatever will I do?"

"Have you consummated the marriage? I know I should not ask such a personal question, but is there a chance of an annulment?" Lady Brandon asked, concern masking her voice.

"There is no chance of an annulment. Most definitely not a route that I can take to fix what I have unwillingly done."

Her ladyship sighed, reaching out to take her hand. "Then it would seem that you're the Duchess of St. Albans. Whatever will you do? Will you confront him with this?"

"I will face him, yes. He has lied to me most cruelly." The idea that she would unwittingly marry the very man who ruined her cousin's life was unfathomable. Of all the people she thought she would meet abroad, he was not one of them. For years, the duke's younger brother had been rumored to be living in Spain, content to stay there and live off the family fortune. Had he been in Italy all this time instead? It would seem that he had.

"I shall walk you to the door and have your carriage summoned if you wish."

"Thank you, yes." Molly couldn't imagine what she was going to say to Hugh. How would she face him knowing who he really was? A stranger she did not know, not really. The forthcoming confrontation left a hollow feeling in her chest and dread to pool in her stomach. How did one leave a marriage? The idea was too awful to contemplate.

≈

*M*olly found Hugh in his tablinum upon her return to the villa. She shut the door and poured herself a well-needed brandy before seating herself across from him. His eyes followed her, hungry and burning with appreciation.

Normally his heady intent would have her slipping onto his lap to let him do as he wished, but not tonight and possibly never again. The idea of not being with him, her Mr. Armstrong, her husband making love to her, and spending time and doing all the things they had planned made her want to scream at the universe.

"Good evening, wife. How did you enjoy the ball? You did not stay overly long. Is everything well?"

She downed her drink, slamming the crystal glass onto his desk. "I did not enjoy it at all, unfortunately."

He sat back in his chair, and the heat that was banked in his eyes a moment before was replaced with unease. "Why is that? Did something happen?"

Molly shook her head, the image of her cousin and her small child dead in their coffin rising up in her mind like a ghoul. How could he have treated them like that? As if they were not worthy of his name and protection. How could she have married the very man who had ruined her cousin's life and the lives of her relatives? They had been devastated by the death of their only daughter. To this day, her aunt's wailing screams when Laura passed from this world would haunt her for the rest of her days.

She bit back tears, schooling her features. "I'm curious, Hugh, just what I should call you. Mr. Armstrong, whom I married, Lord Farley after what I was told this evening, His Grace, the Duke of St. Albans? Perhaps Duke will suffice since we're on intimate terms."

"Hugh will be just fine." His voice held an edge of steel, and she wanted to bend that metal rod, twist it, so it was no longer so rigid and unforgivable.

"You're Lord Farley? Now the Duke of St. Albans. I do not understand."

"I am now." He nodded, raising his brow. "You've heard of my family?"

She scoffed, wishing she did not know of his family as well as she did, but that was never to be. The past had occurred, the horrors along with it, and there was no changing that. "Lord Hugh Farley fled England after he was accused of dallying with an heiress, getting a child onto her, and leaving her to face the *ton's* wrath. Alone."

He didn't say anything, merely watched her in silence,

and the urge to throw something at him, break his calm visage, overwhelmed her. Molly clasped the handles of the chair, forcing herself to not move.

"Did you ruin Miss Laura Cox, Hugh?"

"Who told you that I did? Lady Brandon? She is no reliable source, and I would not believe everything that she has to say."

"I've known Rose for some years, and trust her word. Stop hesitating. Are you the one who society cast out due to your actions toward Laura?"

A muscle worked in his jaw. His lips thinned. "I am the very man who was forced to leave England over the scandal. But not everything is as it seems, Molly. Allow me to explain, and you may think differently."

Molly slapped a hand over her mouth, having heard enough. "See things differently." She stood. "You must be jesting. I will never see anything of that situation other than what occurred. You slept with my cousin, ruined her, and then left her for dead. She did die by the way, during the birth of your son. Did you know that?"

He stared at her, his eyes wide, his face draining of color. "Laura was your cousin? But your last name was Clare. I knew Miss Cox in town, and not once did I see you with her."

"My uncle made his fortune importing and exporting goods from India, he married my father's sister. My father is a vicar. A modest life and income, and because I was a few years younger than Laura, when her fall from grace occurred, I was sent away to France to school. To remove me from the scandal and to keep my reputation safe."

"We were both sent away. I'm sorry for what happened to Laura, but let me explain my side of events. You will see that I'm innocent in all this."

Molly strode to the door. A chair scraped behind her, and before she could open the door but an inch, Hugh was behind her, slamming it shut. She turned, glaring at him. "I married the one man my family and I swore to curse for the rest of our days. How can I return home and tell my parents, aunt, and uncle, that I have slept with our enemy? The very man who ruined a woman's life. You left her to die. For days she suffered in childbirth, and not one word from you."

"You do not know what you speak," he said frowning. "I cared for Laura as a friend, but that is all. I did not do what you accuse me of."

"Really, then tell me, Your Grace, who did? Your elder brother, perhaps? You cannot think that I would believe that your mother would go about society as she did, sorrowful and apologetic for her younger son's actions. No mother would throw the blame on one child over the other, especially if they were innocent of the charge."

He scoffed, running a hand through his hair and leaving it on end. "You did not know my mother." The words were self-derogatory, and she hated that this was what was happening to them.

"You go by the name Mr. Armstrong?" she asked, needing clarification.

"It's my mother's maiden name and not commonly known. A vicar's daughter would not know the intimate details of a duke's marriage that took place years before, now would she?"

The words were cutting, and Molly felt the nick of his tongue's blade just as severe as if he'd cut her with the physical object himself. So, now she was not good enough for him? Not high enough on the social ladder to circulate and know the Duke of St. Albans intimate details?

"I will pack my things and be gone by the morning."

"The hell you will." He glared at her, his eyes narrowing in anger, and yet fear, not hate lurked in his dark depths. Not that it would change her mind. He could not keep her here, no matter what he said or thought. She would return to England and forget her few weeks in Italy.

Or at least try and forget her time here.

Her heart ached at the very thought of it.

"You cannot stop me, Hugh. I will leave you and be gone by morning. Nothing you say or do will change that fact." The thought of their farce marriage near crumbled her resolve to remain strong. "We're not even married. All this time I've been living in sin and with a man I do not even know."

"We are married. I signed the register St. Albans, not Armstrong."

"That does not make it legal," she seethed, blinking to stem her tears. "In a court of law, I highly doubt that would make our marriage legitimate."

A muscle worked in his jaw as he thought over her words. "We will marry again. Without the guise of Armstrong."

She shook her head. Who was this man? "I will not marry Lord Farley, not now or ever. I'm returning to England."

"And so that is all I deserve. You choose to believe I am capable of such a crime and do not believe me when I tell you otherwise."

Molly crossed her arms. She wanted to go to him, to soothe the hurt in his voice, the pain etched on his handsome visage. But she could not. Her cousin's image, cold in her coffin, her little child laying in her arms, put paid to that notion. "What is your side, then, Your Grace? Do, please, enlighten me."

He growled, stalked to the fire where he fisted his hands on the marble mantle. "I never touched Miss Cox. My brother courted her during her first Season, made her believe she was loved and his favorite. Henry had many favorites, your cousin was merely one of them."

Molly listened, not liking that he sounded like he truly believed the words coming out of his mouth. Had she married a madman? A liar? Society would certainly say she'd married a rogue who had ruined an innocent woman and left her to face the *ton's* wrath. Laura certainly had paid the ultimate price for giving her heart to a man.

"Henry got her with child, and when she demanded he do the right thing by her, he threw her aside. Laura threatened Henry in a letter to my mother. A mistake she would live to regret. No one tells the Duke of St. Albans what to do."

She narrowed her eyes, the arrogance of the man, of his family. "She was an heiress, more than suitable for your family. I'm sorry, Your Grace, but the notion behind your excuse is absurd. For years, you've been living abroad, people know it only to be you that was shunned out of society, not your brother. I do not believe you."

"I took the fall, Molly. That is all. I was forced to leave England for the sake of the family image. I prefer Rome in any case, and I've been happy here. But now, as a married man, I know that my life has been missing one important element. You."

"Well, you shall miss that element again, for I am not staying. I cannot believe the Duke of Whitstone is your friend. Once he finds out that Laura was my cousin, I doubt you'll have even him as your supporter."

"Did you hear a word that I said?"

"I did," she said, "and I do not believe it. No one would leave their homeland, take the fall for anyone, not even for their brother." She glanced about the room, the well-stocked shelves of books, the leather chairs before the fire, and mahogany desk. The opulence that she'd never noticed before. Of course, she knew he was not struggling, but she had not seen everything as clearly as she now did. "They paid you to leave. Guilty or not, you choose money over honor." She rushed for the door.

"Molly, wait." He clasped her arm, and she shook off his hold.

Molly held up her hand, trying to gather all the tidbits of information as she knew them. "Say your brother did dishonor my cousin, you still chose to leave England. To live abroad and in the same type of lifestyle that you enjoyed back home. Instead of forcing your brother to do the right thing, making him marry Laura, you ran away. Like a coward."

He swallowed, his skin a deathly gray. "I had no choice, Molly. Please believe me that I did try. I know you do not believe me, but I did fight for Laura. Henry would not be moved, and my mother even more so. Do not leave me. I cannot live without you."

Her eyes burned with unshed tears, and she sniffed, not wanting him to see her cry. "You did not try hard enough. I do not know who you are."

He clasped her arms, pinning her before him. His hands shook, and she willed herself to be strong. To not be swayed. "You do know who I am. More than anyone else. Do you believe I could act so callously toward a woman? For all your sweetness and how much I love you, you are not nobility. I did not have to marry you if I did not choose to. I love you, fell in love with you, and want to spend the rest of my life with you. No title, not even a ducal one, could stop me from having you forever, and it did not.

"When we took our vows, I said mine as the Duke of St. Albans. The registrar is signed with St. Albans, not Armstrong. Why would I have not married your cousin had I loved her? She was an heiress, some would say more suitable than you were for my rank. It was not me, Molly. I was not the man behind your cousin's downfall."

She pushed him away, having heard enough. "I do not know what I believe, but what I do know is that everyone believes it was you, even your mother. You ran away to Italy and hid here for years like some sort of criminal. How am I to just dismiss all of that? I cannot."

"You're making a mistake."

She turned and reached for the door, wrenching it open. "Maybe I am, but know this, you allowed me to marry you when so much of your past was hidden. Like a thief in the night, you concealed why you left London and your true name. Even if my cousin was not involved, you seem to be so very comfortable living a lie that it sends shivers up my spine."

"I intended to tell you the truth. I just could not find the right time. I'm sorry that I did not."

Molly scoffed, glancing at him over the shoulder. "Hindsight is a wonderful thing, is it not? If only we could do things over again, perhaps we would've acted differently, but I suppose we shall never know now." She walked from the room, leaving Hugh behind. She would return to London tomorrow first thing, return to England, and figure out her life without her husband.

A man she had thought she knew, loved with all her heart. Worse, however, would be when she faced her family. When they found out who she had married, they would never forgive her. They, too, would shun her and demand she leave them be. The thought sent a pulse of revulsion to course through her body, and she ran the last few steps to her room, just making it and retching into her chamber pot. She slumped against the wall, spent and nauseated. No more fitting end to a wretched night could she have asked for. Perfect.

CHAPTER 12

London - One month later

*M*olly returned to London a few weeks into the new Season. Her trip made less arduous and long due to Lord Brandon allowing her the use of his ship to escort her back to London. A welcome reprieve due to her stomach ailing her the whole time she was at sea. Molly had put her infirmity down to her churning stomach. Her thoughts taunting and mocking that she was returning home without her husband. That Hugh had not attempted to stop her the morning she left was a hurt that ripped her in half and would never heal.

How could he have sat in his office, staring at his paperwork, not bothering to look up as she passed his door? Molly wasn't sure what hurt her the most. That he was a liar, a man who had fled England after ruining her cousin, or that he couldn't care one whit that she was leaving him. Did not a man who declared he was in love with her, not fight to keep her heart? How could he have been so cold and aloof when inside her chest, her heart broke into a million pieces?

She sat in the parlor in the house her good friend Marchioness Ryley owned. A home Willow used to share with Molly and Evie until they married and went on with their new lives. The Duke of Albans' man of business had called in on her only yesterday, offering her the ducal property on Grosvenor square. He stated the house was fully staffed and at her disposal should she wish to use it. She merely only need travel there.

She would not be going anywhere near the London home or the duke's country estate. Neither home held any interest to her. Although at times, she had found herself driving past the house in town and looking at it, marveling at the grand Georgian design, the pillars and house frontage that had its own carriage entrance off the square.

A silly little fool who needed to remember why she left her husband in the first place.

Guilt pricked her soul each time she thought of who she was now. No longer Miss Molly Clare, but the Duchess of St. Albans. A traitor to her family, to her cousin. Even though she had not been aware of her wrongdoing, it still did not make her current circumstances right.

A light knock on the door sounded, and her footman announced the Duchess of Carlisle.

"Evie!" Molly stood, all but running to her friend to pull her into a tight embrace. "I'm so very happy to see you. Please tell me you are now arrived in town and are here to stay."

Evie hugged her back, before pulling her over to a nearby settee. Before sitting, she rang for tea, and came and sat beside her. "We are here for the remainder of the

Season. I was so eager to return to town when I heard you were back from Rome. I also heard quite a remarkable rumor that you need to explain to me before my curiosity drives me to bedlam."

Molly knew only too well what rumor had brought Evie around to her home. Still, she was curious just how inquisitive she was. "When did you arrive in London?"

"Only just now. I had the carriage drop me here. Finn continued on to our townhouse." Evie adjusted her seat, meeting her gaze. "You traveled to Rome for an adventure, and from what I hear, you had quite a significant one. How are you faring being a Duchess?"

Molly sighed, slumping into her chair. "Not very well at all. I've made the most dreadful mistake, and I do not know what I shall do."

Concern replaced Evie's amused visage. She frowned. "Why is marriage to the Duke of St. Albans so very bad? He's rumored to be immensely handsome, not to mention rich. You'll be beholden to no one, not even your family. That is a good thing, is it not?"

Molly knew all too well how handsome Hugh was, and loving. The many mornings waking up in his arms had been the most wonderful of her life. His wicked grins that still made her stomach flip, her blood to heat. Even knowing the truth of his past. Her heart broke while her mind screamed to stay strong, to not forgive.

"Do you remember hearing of Lord Farley and his expulsion from London society and England some years ago? He ruined Miss Laura Cox."

A puzzled look crossed Evie's brow before she said, "I believe so. He fled to Spain the last I heard. Why is this relevant to your marriage?"

A tear slipped down her cheek, and she swiped it away. Annoyed that after all these weeks without Hugh, she was still emotional about everything. His conduct. Her leaving. So many things left unsaid.

Lord Hugh Farley was the Duke of St. Albans' younger brother." Molly met Evie's eyes and watched as comprehension dawned on her features.

"What? No, it could not be. You married the scoundrel that ruined that poor girl? Even his family turned against him. She was an heiress, perfectly acceptable really to marry a duke's second son, but he refused. How is it that your paths even crossed?"

"He was not in Spain, and he never went by the name Farley in Rome, but Armstrong. His mother's name apparently. Worse is yet to be spoken, however, Evie. So much worse." Her stomach twisted, and she took a calming breath, relieved when a servant brought in the tea and some ginger biscuits.

"I will pour, thank you," the Duchess of Carlisle said, dismissing the footman.

Molly took the tea and sighed in delight as the sweet brew met her tongue. She picked up a ginger biscuit and nibbled.

"Tell me what could possibly be worse than marrying that man?" Evie asked.

Molly sipped again, steeling herself to say the words that haunted her conscience. "Miss Laura Cox, the heiress whom my husband ruined all those years ago, is my cousin. My father and her mother are siblings. They were well-to-do. My uncle was business savvy and earned his fortune and climbed up into the society in which he wished Laura to marry. My father is a vicar, and so we circulated in different circles. When Laura fell from grace, I was packed off to France, where I would be safe from such rakehells."

"Oh, my dear Molly. I do not know what to say. That is, I have a lot to say, but I cannot believe how unfortunate this all is. What did His Grace say about Laura? How did he explain his actions toward her?"

"He said it wasn't him that ruined her, but in fact his brother, he merely took the fall. I do not believe him, of course. Now that his brother is dead, there is no one to naysay him."

"True," Evie said, biting her lip in thought. "But what if it is true? Is there a chance that he may be innocent?"

"I do not think so. His mother, the duchess even pulled away from him over his actions. No mother would turn away from her child, surely. You defend your children, love them and guide them as best you can."

"Not all mothers are created equal. From what I remember of the Duchess of St. Albans she was a taxing, haranguing woman who enjoyed belittling people she did not like. I do not think she would have been the most loving parent."

"Perhaps not, but it does not change what her son is accused of. Hugh told me himself that he knew Laura, he said that he'd tried to convince his brother to marry her, but was unsuccessful."

"So not entirely terrible, if he's telling the truth, that is," Evie said, her tone placating.

"Even if he's innocent of the crime, he allowed his family to let him take the fall. He was sent abroad, with all life's little luxuries that were not afforded to Laura. He's lived a full and happy life in Rome. Laura was buried at only twenty years of age."

"Oh, Molly, that is very sad. Whatever will you do?"

Molly stood, going to a nearby decanter and pouring herself a good serving of brandy. She downed it quickly, before pouring another. "I do not know. I married a Mr. Armstrong, not the Duke of St. Albans. I'm not even certain our marriage is legitimate, even though Hugh said he signed the register St. Albans."

Evie stared at her, eyes wide in shock. "So you may not even be married?"

Molly chewed her lip, frowning. "Possibly not." She paused. "To society we appear married, there is a register of our marriage, it was only the vows that were misspoken. I cannot let anyone know the truth. If they were to find out that our marriage may not have been legitimate, I will have ruined myself and brought more shame onto my family than I can bear."

"I agree. It is best that no one is told of your unusual wedding." Evie placed her teacup and saucer down, studying her a moment. "Where is St. Albans? Has he returned to England?"

"No," Molly said, hating that her heart panged at the thought of him being so very far away. "Hugh is still in Rome. It is unlikely he will return given our parting."

"And the ginger biscuits? How do they factor into all of this? Is there yet another secret you are keeping?" Evie asked, meeting her gaze.

Molly instinctively reached to cradle her stomach and the new little life that she grew there. A child made with love who would now grow up never knowing his or her father. Molly could only pray that it was a girl. To deliver an heir to the St. Albans line before she was certain their marriage was legitimate would be a disaster. After their cold parting, his declarations of love and affection toward her must not have been as sincere as she thought. There would be no second marriage to legitimize their union, even if she had wanted one, which she did not.

"The doctor has told me I'm *enceinte*. There are only a few weeks left of the Season, and I'm not showing a great deal. I do not think anyone will notice." Molly glanced down at her stomach, the small little bump hidden mostly from the material of her gown.

"Now that I know, I can tell, but the biscuits gave you away, my dear. Even so, you were married, and there is no shame in you having a baby by the duke. You must take up your position in the St. Albans townhouse with the belief that the marriage is legitimate. Your child will need to grow up in the homes he or she will inherit."

"I cannot go there. I would feel like a hypocrite. My family would never speak to me again should I take up residence there. In the home that has caused my family so much pain." Another tear slid free, and she dabbed at it with the back of her hand, annoyed she found herself in such a position. Her trip to Rome had been going so well, she had adored every minute exploring the country. For all of it to come to a dreadful end wasn't to be borne. The blow of leaving Rome was bad enough, nevertheless having to face the fact the man that she loved with all her heart had ripped hers from her chest and seemed perfectly content to let her leave without a by your leave.

How could he have let her go so easily?

"You must and soon." Evie paused, pursing her lips. "Has there been any communication from the duke or his steward regarding your position in society now?"

"His steward came here only a few days ago, notifying me that I may move into the St. Albans townhouse whenever I wish. No news from Hugh, however, but that does not surprise me."

"Why ever not? If you were my wife, I would move heaven and earth to be by your side. To try to win you back."

Molly lifted her lips into a semblance of a smile at her dear friend's words. She sat next to her again, reaching over to take her hand. "I know you would, but you love me as much as I love you. Hugh obviously does not love me as much as I thought he did."

"How could he not? You're the most perfect person I know."

Molly nodded, wishing that were true. If she had been more perfect, she would not have married the enemy. Or taken part in a fictional marriage either. What a fool she was. "There are too many things between us to make our union work, no matter how much I enjoyed his company."

"You enjoyed more than his company. I can see it in your eyes that you were in love with him. You miss him, do you not?"

Evie had always been able to read Molly better than any of their other friends. Molly was closest to Evie within their friendship group, but she did wish she could not pick up on such nuances. The thought of not seeing Hugh again left a crater in her chest where her heart once beat.

For the small amount of time that they were together, she'd fallen in love with her husband. Had given in to his every wish, his every whim. One look from his piercing gaze, banked with a fire and need made her biddable and willing.

For the rest of her life, she would be without him, unable to hear his voice or his touch. She swallowed the bile that rose in her throat. There was a reason why, of course, that she had to remove herself from his life. He was a seducer of innocent women. A man who ruined the life of her cousin. She could not simply sweep the past away that had affected so much of her upbringing, simply because she loved him. She loved the man she thought he was, not the man who he actually was. Had she known he was the Duke of St. Albans' younger brother, she would never have stayed at his Roman villa. Never have given him the time to get to know her.

"When is Ava coming to town? I need to speak to her. She cannot possibly know that the villa they offered to me while in Rome was Lord Farley's. Surely the duke would not have thrown me into the path of a man shadowed by a terrible scandal."

"Ava and Tate are not due in town for another week. They're holding a ball Thursday next. You should have to wait until then to speak to her, I should imagine."

Molly chewed her lip, thinking. "I suppose I should have to, but it does seem odd, does it not? I'm one of their closest friends. Surely they would not put me in such a difficult position."

"Did they know Miss Cox was your cousin?" Evie asked.

"No," she admitted. "No one knows that we were related, but they must have known that Hugh was involved. Unless they, too, do not believe the duke's brother and mother who accused him of the crime. They would not be so foolhardy, do you think?"

Evie picked up her tea and took a sip. "We shall not know the truth until they return, and I do not want you fussing over the answer to that question until you know the truth. Ava would never intentionally hurt you. I believe there is a simple explanation to your dilemma."

Molly hoped it was so. She slumped back into the settee's soft velvet, not quite believing that her life which had been going so perfectly well was now a complete mess.

"I shall talk to her at the ball, you're right. Until then, I will try to forget about everything."

"I think that is best, my dear. Now, tell me of the sights of Rome and the continent. I want to know everything."

CHAPTER 13

*M*olly had kept busy over the days leading up to the Duke and Duchess of Whitstone's ball by ordering a new gown and writing letters to her parents, aunt, and uncle, inviting them to London to stay with her.

If anyone had information regarding Laura and what happened that fateful Season, it was her aunt Jossalin. Surely they knew the truth or at least could help her in finding out what had occurred instead of hearsay.

She was not looking forward to explaining her actions, of how her marriage to the Duke of St. Albans had come about or how much she'd loved him. Molly could well understand how her cousin had fallen for such sweet words and exquisite touches that Hugh could bestow for she had crumbled like a biscuit under his touch. Blotting the missive, she stared down at the parchment and prayed that her family would understand she had been blind to his past. That they would forgive her.

It never occurred to Molly that the one man who made her blood sing would be the very one they had cursed to the devil years ago. The very thought of confronting her aunt with her mistake made her stomach churn.

~

*L*ater that evening was her first foray into London society. Evie and her husband, the Duke of Carlisle, had picked her up in their carriage, and it had taken minutes only to pull up before the Duke and Duchess of Whitstone's grand London townhouse.

The moment her name was announced, the room abuzz with conversation, music, and laughter noticeably quietened. Molly clasped her fan tighter, cooling her skin to stem from the never-ending sickness that ailed her. She raised her chin, not willing for any of them to look down at her or judge her choice.

Molly reminded herself they did not know that she was Laura's cousin, that the connection had thankfully never been made. It was only by chance that Lady Brandon had found out. She was certain no one else would know.

To imagine what they would think and say should they know the duke had married the cousin of the woman he ruined all those years ago sent a shudder of revulsion down her spine. The *ton* would then roar with ridicule, mock and criticize. She was not sure she could weather that storm as well.

"My darling, there is something that I need to speak to you about," Willow whispered to her as she joined them, pulling her toward where Hallie and Ava stood with their respective husbands.

Molly shot a look at Willow, not liking her taut tone. "What is it that you need to say? Is there something the matter?"

"There is news that you must know."

They came to stand before Ava and Hallie. She kissed them both in turn, greeting the dukes standing at their wives' backs, before turning toward the gathered throng. Willow worked her hands before her, glancing at the door. Hallie pulled her aside, and dread pooled in her stomach. "Willow, what is wrong?"

The hair on the back of her nape rose as the muttering of voices dimmed. The music fell as conversation quietened. Molly forgot her question to her friend and looked to see what had everyone so fascinated.

The booming voice of the major-domo bellowed out the name of the latest guest. "His Grace, the Duke of St. Albans."

Molly stilled, her body seized with panic. Hugh was in London. Willow clasped her hand, squeezing it a little. Molly searched him out in the crowded room, but she could not see him. Was it really Hugh? Was he back in London?

A small part of her mind screamed it was because he was here for her. That he'd come to repair their broken marriage, but there was little he could do. The past, no matter how many apologies one gave out, could not change what had occurred.

Unless he is innocent of the crime.

Molly pushed the unhelpful thought aside. He was guilty, had fled London to escape the *ton's* censure. No one innocent acted in such a way.

"That is what I wanted to tell you. Your husband has arrived in London, and from what I heard from Abe, he was at Whites Gentleman's club today with the Duke of Whitstone. His Grace was overheard telling Whitstone he was in town to win back his wife."

Oh, dear Lord. Did that mean all of society knew that they had a falling out? It was no secret what his scandalous past incurred, and now they knew she had scurried back to England from Rome. She could only imagine what the *ton* was saying about them both behind closed doors.

Heat rose on her neck.

"You've gone very pale, my dear. Are you well?" Ava took her hand, patting it a little.

Thoughts of what the Duke of St. Albans and his family did to hers rushed back into her mind and made the room spin. Of her cousin who had been courted and promised things during her coming-out by Hugh. How all of those things had come to nothing, not after receiving what he wanted all along. Her innocence and nothing else.

"Ava, did you know Mr. Armstrong was Lord Farley when you saw me off to Rome?"

Her friend's brow furrowed, a grim look on her face. "I did not, no, my dear. Tate has explained his absence to me since your return, and I know my husband, Molly, he would not lie nor support a liar. He believes St. Albans to be telling the truth."

"Did he see Hugh's brother demand he take the fall for him?" To have been a witness would at least clear Hugh of that offense.

Ava shook her head. "No, he read the missive that was sent to Lord Farley from his family."

Hope bloomed in her heart that perhaps Hugh could prove his innocence after all. "Well then, Hugh just needs to show me that letter so I can see for myself what was asked of him. Not that it changes the fact he went along with such a heartbreaking ruse."

"I'm sorry, Molly, but you cannot. So enraged was Hugh by the demand, the letter was burned that very night. You will not be able to read it, my dear. I'm so sorry." Ava stepped back, joining her husband, who looked sheepish at best.

She swallowed her nerves at facing Hugh again. There was nothing he could say that could change what she thought of his conduct. But blast it all to hades, he looked dashing.

She watched, along with every other woman in the room, as the Roman god of sin strode across the ballroom floor. Gone were his tan breeches and cravet-less shirt that he often wore in Rome, and in its place was a man made for ogling. For pleasure and all wicked, delicious things. His eyes bored into her, never diverting to anyone else, and for the life of her, she could not look away. She ought to run, her mind certainly screamed to flee, but she could not. A small part of her wanted to hear what he had to say. How he would explain away his actions. He'd tried in Rome, and he had failed. He would fail again here.

"I'm so sorry, Molly. I can only imagine what you are feeling." Evie clasped her hand, standing beside her and facing down the duke like a knight going into battle.

"Oh dear," Evie whispered, the words rushing from her the closer he came. "He is a marvelous specimen."

Molly's breath hitched, and a sheen of sweat broke out on her brow. She took a calming breath, needing to compose herself for the inevitable confrontation. She had not thought to see him again. Had thought he would stay in Rome as he said he would.

The Duke of Whitstone and Carlisle stepped in front of Molly and came to greet Hugh. Molly watched them, the genuine accord and friendship shone through all of their eyes. Betrayal coursed through her blood. How could they be friends with a man who had caused her family so much harm? Molly reminded herself that they did not know Laura was her cousin. A fact she would soon amend.

Worse still, how could she still love that very man?

Molly blinked back the burn of tears. She no longer loved him, to do so would be the veriest perfidy. The three dukes, the highest nobles of the realm before royalty, stood together, laughing and talking as if they had not spent the past ten years apart. All the while, Molly felt the scorch of Hugh's eyes on her. His gaze slid across her person, from her head to her toes and back again like a physical caress.

Her breasts felt heavy and large in her gown. With every breath, her bodice's silk rippled across her nipples that were already sensitive from the child she carried in her womb. She supposed she would have to tell him that she was *enceinte*. So many things they needed to discuss, to plan on how they would continue this marriage apart.

A shadow fell before her, and she took her attention off the dancers and met Hugh's stare head on. He picked up her gloved hand, never averting his attention before kissing her. "Duchess." The title slipped from his lips like a caress, a declaration of fact, and one from the measured tone of his voice he intended to keep as truth.

"Your Grace," she answered, glad that her voice didn't wobble like her knees beneath her gown. She dipped into a curtsy, allowing him to keep her hand in his as he came to stand beside her. Had he stopped her from leaving Rome, they could have had this conversation there, worked out the particulars of their union. But no, he had to choose the very first ball that she attended in London to have it out with her.

"I've missed you." The whisper of his words tickled her ear, and she fought not to shiver. How could she be tempted by such a man? A seducer of women, and one who would let them suffer the consequences of those erotic actions. "We need to talk." His hand shifted to wrap about her waist, his fingers taking a long time to settle on her hip.

"What if I do not want to talk to you?" Molly did not dare glance at him. To stare at such beauty would only end with her being blind to his actions. She needed more time to compose herself and prepare for their confrontation. They could not have it here, at the Whitstone's ball. That would never do.

The sounds of a waltz started to play, and couples hurried out onto the dancefloor. The duke clasped her hand, pulling her along with them. Molly followed, not wanting to make a scene. She smiled, looking to all the world as a woman who was gleefully happy her husband was going to dance with her. The truth could not be more opposed.

He swung her into his arms, too close for her comfort. Molly tried to step away, put a little space between them, but she may have been trying to shift a limb of a tree for all the good her actions did. "You're holding me too tight, Duke."

His wicked grin made her countenance slip, and she narrowed her eyes. He chuckled. "So much fire in your veins. I have missed you, my darling love."

Her heart gave a thump at his words. Damn him and his sweet endearments. His playing with her was cruel and unkind. "You can no longer call me your darling love. I am not."

One brow rose with a disbelieving air. "Are you certain, my darling love? I know that my feelings have not changed from the moment you abandoned me in Rome."

"I did not abandon you, I left you perfectly capable of looking after yourself with your staff. Has your memory failed you so miserably that you cannot remember why I left in the first place?"

"Oh, I remember, and I'm in London to ensure you believe the truth, if not from my lips, then from those who know what really happened."

Molly shot a look at Hugh, a little glimmer of hope taking light inside her that there may be someone who knew what really happened. As much as she wished she could believe him, her family had thought Laura's lover was Hugh. Why would anyone lie about such a thing? Her aunt and uncle would never have made up such a falsehood.

The dance pulled them into a couple of tight turns, and his clutch increased, keeping her locked against his person. Her body purred in response as if it remembered what he made her feel, wanting more of the same. She could not give in to his seductive charms. Not without knowing the truth behind his banishment. What she needed to do was speak to her aunt and uncle.

"I have ordered your staff to pack your things to move into St. Albans London house. Your place is with me."

She huffed out a breath—the audacity of the man. "I will not be going anywhere with you. As far as I still understand, you ruined my cousin and left without a backward glance. Agreed to funds over honor. I'm surprised that you're here in London at all. When I left Rome, I had the distinct feeling that I knew what my cousin went through when you let her go without a fight."

"I never ruined your cousin. Why will you not believe me?" She swallowed, sensing his visage of an aloof, sanguine gentleman was slipping. "It was not me who laid one finger on your cousin. It was my brother." A muscle worked in his jaw, and he stared at her, hard. Frustration burned in his stormy gaze.

Molly wished she could believe him, wished she had not lived for years, knowing another tale. Somewhere between the start of their dance and their conversation, they had stopped dancing. Out of her peripheral vision, she could see other couples continued to waltz about them. "I'm sorry, Hugh, but I do not know whom to believe."

"If we're to stay as we were in Rome, I need you to trust me."

"Trust you? You did not even marry me using your real name. How can I trust you? If you were not trying to hide your identity, why did you not tell me the truth? All of it, the weeks we spent together look like a falsehood now. How can I trust you ever again?"

"First, I signed the marriage register with St. Albans, you just did not notice it. Second, I would not be in London, having the *ton* gossip and sneer behind my back unless what I said was the truth. Unless I knew they were wrong, and I was right. My friends, the Duke of Whitstone and Duncannon believe me, but you do not. I do not understand it. I thought you loved me. Was that a misunderstanding on my behalf?"

The music faded to a stop, and she pulled out of his hold and strode for the entrance hall. She needed to leave. How could he ask her such a question? He knew as well as herself how much she adored and loved him. To be angry with her made no sense. It was not she who had done the wrong thing. He had. A youth at the time or not, did not excuse his actions.

He caught up to her in the foyer as a footman was handing her her pelisse. Hugh clasped her hand, calling for his carriage.

"I can have a Hackney cab called. I do not need you to return me to my home."

"The hell I'll allow my duchess to travel in a hackney." The black, highly polished carriage rolled to a halt before the townhouse's front steps. Hugh held out his hand to assist her into the vehicle, and she ignored his proffered hand, climbing up herself.

He followed, calling for St. Albans house. She scowled at him across the shadowy space that separated them. "I'm not staying at Grosvenor Square. You cannot make me."

"I can, and you will. Whether you love me anymore, trust, or believe me, St. Albans House is where its duchess resides. You will be safe there, be well cared for when I return to Rome."

She could not look at him when he mentioned such things. So he intended to leave her? Of course, he would, if she could not believe or love him as she had in Rome, what was left for him in London? Her heart ached at the very idea of Hugh living so very far away from her. If her aunt confirmed Hugh as the one who had ruined Laura, what was she to do? The man she fell in love with in Italy was honorable, sweet, and kind. So very loving to her, at least.

Her cousin had been played the fool, so how could she forgive such treatment to soothe her own selfish wants and needs from the same man? An older, more mature Hugh than Laura obviously knew. An impossible choice.

"Very well, I shall stay at St. Albans House, but until I know who is telling me the truth and who is not, I do not wish to live as husband and wife. Please do not expect me to open my apartment doors to you. I will not."

His eyes flashed with annoyance, and for the life of her she could not look away. To stay away from her husband would be a chore, Molly had no doubt about that. Her body yearned for his touch, his lips on her flesh, what his clever hands and mouth could do that sent her pulse to race. Her core ached at the memory of their last coming together, and she crossed her arms over her chest.

"When you learn the truth, my love, and you will, I expect recompense for the time that I've had to live without you."

She scoffed at him. "And if you are proven to be the ruiner of young, unmarried women, what do I get? Oh, let me tell you. A farcical marriage to a man who will live hundreds of miles away from me and I stuck with society forever laughing at me that I had been fool enough to marry the man who ruined my cousin."

"They do not know Miss Cox was your cousin. And anyway, I am right, and you are wrong, so it will all work out in the end."

"It will only be a matter of time before they do know Laura was a relation." She shook her head. "You're so very sure you'll be proven innocent."

He leaned forward, his beautiful features coming more into focus as they rumbled through the London streets. "Do you not wish to see me proven innocent? You seem determined to believe everyone else except me."

Molly wanted to reach out, soothe the hurt she could read in his eyes, but she did not. Instead, she slumped back onto the squabs and watched the passing houses in Mayfair go by. "I have invited my aunt and uncle to stay. If anyone knows the truth it is them, and then I shall know how to act."

CHAPTER 14

The following weeks in the St. Albans house were not a comfortable existence, certainly not for Hugh. His wife went about her days, paying calls, visiting her close friends, and hosting them in return. Outwardly, the *ton* believed that they were a happily married couple. That Miss Molly Clare had tamed the rogue Lord Hugh Farley, now Duke of St. Albans, but they would be wrong.

Their close friends knew the truth of the situation. That when they were home, Molly barely spoke to him, spent her days in the warm, sunny parlor at the back of the house while he whiled away his hours in the library at the front.

He hated their separation and would do anything to correct the wrong. Molly had come to him and told him that next week her aunt and uncle would be traveling to town to see her. To discuss what they knew.

Molly's family had not taken the news of their marriage well, and her parents had refused to attend, to come along with her aunt and uncle. Hugh knew the slight hurt Molly. She had been close with her parents. To have them turn their backs on her now, left a rage to simmer in his blood.

No one gave the cut direct to the Duchess of St. Albans and got away with it.

Hugh leaned back in the leather-bound chair behind his desk, his mind frantic on how he could prove to her his innocence. He had hoped to speak to his late brother's valet, who was privy to all the duke's whereabouts and had known of his liaison with Miss Cox, but returning to London, he'd found out that he'd been killed along with his brother in the carriage accident.

And now he was fucked. How was he going to prove that it hadn't been him, he was merely the brother, the spare who had taken the blame? The letter his mother had sent too was no use, for the fool that he was, he'd burned the blasted thing in a fit of rage.

Over the last two weeks, he'd watched his wife with a longing that both frustrated and vexed him. He'd never been a man who could not live without a woman. His life up to meeting Molly had been full, entertaining, and had its shares of liaisons too, but it was different now. He wanted her trust, her love. To have her back in his arms where he knew true happiness and contentment.

The ducal bed was vast and cold as it now lay. He wanted her back in it, to be with him.

"Your Grace, the duchess," a servant puffed, sliding into the library on the polished parquetry floor, his breathing ragged from running. "She has collapsed in the back parlor."

Hugh shot to his feet, running past the pale and wide-eyed servant as he raced to the parlor Molly liked to use. He charged into the room, seeing a maid trying to rouse the duchess. Hugh slid down next to her, leaning close to her to hear if she was breathing. A small flutter of breath touched his cheek, and relief washed through him like a balm. She was alive. As long as that were so, all else would be well. "What happened? Was she feeling ill this morning?" he questioned the maid.

She shook her head, frowning. "Her Grace was well when I brought in the tea just now. As I stoked the fire for her, she complained of dizziness and dropped the teacup she was holding. She must have been leaning forward on the chair a little, for she slumped onto the floor."

"Send for a doctor and hurry. I will carry Her Grace to her room."

"Yes, Your Grace," the maid said, dipping into a curtsy.

Hugh reached under Molly and scooped her up in his arms. He carried her to her room, a maid hurrying before him to open her door and pull back the bedding.

Just as he laid her down on the cool linens, she stirred, confusion clouding her features. "What happened?" she asked, looking about her room. "How did I get back into my bedchamber?"

"You swooned in the parlor. I have sent for the doctor. How are you feeling?" He reached out, touching her forehead. She was not warm, it did not seem like there was anything wrong with her outwardly.

"Not again," she mumbled.

Hugh frowned. She'd fainted before today? "This is not the first time you've collapsed?"

"No," she sighed, rubbing her brow. "I found myself on the floor in my room last week, but I'm, well, merely pregnant, Hugh."

Hugh stared at her, slack-jawed. "What?" He stumbled back, running a hand through his hair. He took in his wife, and for the first time, noticed that her stomach was a little bigger than when in Rome. Her breasts too strained against her day gown, and her complexion was pale. "You're what?" Emotion welled up inside him, and he blinked back the burn of tears. He was going to be a father?

She stared at him, patent and calm, a little quirk to her lips. His heart gave a thump. She had not smiled at him at all since his return. "We're having a baby, Hugh. I became ill on the boat back from Rome, and when that illness did not abate, and my courses did not arrive, I knew that I was carrying your child."

"Why did you not send for me?" Pain sliced through him that she would keep such news from him. Did she loathe him so very much that she would deny him the chance to be a father? To teach his child right from wrong. Guide his daughter how to be kind and resourceful and his son, honorable and strong. All the things that his parents failed when it came to his elder brother. His sister Sarah was kind and resourceful, a woman not to be crossed, and he loved her for it, but it had been his father who had taught them what was good in life and how to treat people. His mother had spoiled their older brother and ruined him, made him the man who was now causing all the problems he faced within his marriage.

"I wanted to be sure first, and then the fear that you would not come, would not care to return stopped me. We did not part on the best of terms."

He came over to where she lay and sat. He picked up her hands. They were cold to the touch, and he rubbed them, trying to bring warmth back into her veins. "I know you do not believe me, not many do, my elder brother was a masterful liar and swindler. It was probably why your cousin fell for his false charms so easily. With all that is between us and still to be solved, I will always be here for you, whether you wish me to be or not. I love you, Molly, and I'm going to fight for you until the truth is known."

She squeezed his hand a little, and hope bloomed in his chest. Somehow he'd find someone who knew the truth and clear his name. He would not lose the woman he loved, adored with all his heart over a brother who had brought nothing but pain and cruelty wherever he went. He would not take the one good thing in his life.

His wife.

CHAPTER 15

A week later, Molly sat in her favorite parlor that was for her own personal use and poured her aunt and uncle tea. They had traveled up from the country the day before, opting to stay at a hotel rather than here with her or at their London home where Laura had passed. Her hands shook as she poured the tea, and she hoped they did not notice. She had woken up more ill than normal, her stomach roiling with dread at having to face her family and explain her actions. Try to get them to understand that she had not known that Mr. Armstrong was one and the same as Laura's lover.

If that were the case, after all.

She handed them both a cup of tea and sat, steeling herself for the forthcoming conversation. "Thank you for coming today to see me. I know it's not under the best of circumstances."

Her aunt refused to look at her, and as for her uncle, he stared, a look of contempt shadowing his normally jovial countenance. "We were shocked and saddened to hear of your wedding. Not a statement I thought to utter, but Molly, what were you thinking marrying this bounder?"

Molly swallowed, eschewing that anyone would talk of Hugh in such a way and hating that they may be right. "I married a Mr. Armstrong, not Lord Farley. I did not know Hugh was in any way related to Lord Farley or St. Albans."

"How could you have done this to us? After everything that man did to our family?"

Molly adjusted her seat, her hope that Hugh would be vindicated in his claims to innocence slipping away like the seconds of time. "I did not know, and the marriage was consummated before I found out the truth. I cannot change what is done, but my future happiness relies on what you tell me today. Are you certain that it was the Duke of St. Albans' younger brother that seduced Laura?"

"Why our darling Laura never told us exactly who it was that ruined her, we did find in her bedroom dressing table a small likeness." Her aunt searched through her reticule and pulled out a miniature frame and picture. "Here, this is the likeness with the initials H St. Albans on the back."

Molly took the small painting and immediately viewed a man who very much looked like Hugh, although there were some differences, this gentleman seemed to have more of an aquiline slant to his nose than to Hugh's straight one. His eyes also were smaller, less almond-shaped to Hugh's, beadier. "While they are similar, the H could also stand for Henry, my husband's elder brother."

Her aunt's mouth pinched into a disapproving line. "While we may like to think a duke took an interest in our Laura and courted her, I have little doubt that it was the younger brother who suited her better. A second son could marry an heiress such as Laura, not the heir. And I saw Lord Hugh Farley with Laura at balls and parties, sometimes with their heads together as if they were plotting and planning their futures."

Molly sat back in her chair, taken aback by the idea that Hugh had been close with her cousin, had been, in fact, her lover in truth. Within her own mind, she had decided to find the truth before believing anything else. The idea made her want to cast up her accounts for the second time this morning.

"Could he have been acting on behalf of the duke? Or trying to persuade Laura to look to someone else than his brother? Warn her off, perhaps?" If the duke was anything like Hugh had explained him to Molly, his brother was the worst of people. The other alternative that Hugh had been lying to her, had in fact been Laura's lover was unthinkable.

"May I keep this likeness? I wish to show it to Hugh and ask him if he or his brother is in the image."

"Laura's lover was not the duke," her uncle said, pointing to the small painting in her hands. "Never once did we see the duke with Laura at any balls or assemblies. When Laura confronted the Duchess of St. Albans about her son's actions and the consequences Laura then faced, she promised retribution against her son."

Her aunt dabbed at her cheeks, her eyes welling with tears. "Laura did not confide in us at first, took all this trouble on herself without help. By the time the scandal broke in London, Lord Hugh was banished from England and Laura heavy with his baby. She took his leaving hard, and by the time she had her son, she no longer had the will to live."

"Your husband killed our daughter." Her uncle glowered, his voice wobbly with emotion.

Molly stared at her aunt and uncle, the pain echoing off them still after all these years. That they lost not only Laura but also the babe made her departure from this realm even more devastating.

"Laura was an heiress, why did the Duchess of St. Albans not make Hugh marry her? Why force Laura to hide in the country, and send her son away abroad to live out his days? It makes no sense."

"The duchess was a proud woman, a daughter of a duke herself. She did not believe in the different classes marrying. Not even her younger son would she allow to marry a woman whose inheritance came from trade. Her sons would marry women equal to their birth or no one at all."

For a moment, Molly thought about what the duchess would think of her marriage to Hugh. A vicar's daughter without an ounce of money to her name. A weight settled on her chest, and she took a calming breath. She had loved her cousin. Outside her family, she had been like an older sister, wise and beautiful and always kind. To think that her Hugh had left her to die with a broken heart, in turn, crumbled Molly's heart in her chest.

"Did Laura leave a diary at all? Anything that can, without doubt, prove who the father of her child was?" As small as it was, Molly hung on to any tidbit of chance that Hugh was innocent as he claimed. He had to be. She loved him, was having his child. If she did not find out the truth, forever there would be this divide, a shadow that hung over their union. She could not live like that. She would rather never see him again if that were the case.

"We have not been able to find it. We've searched her

room, everywhere where we thought she would leave such an item, and we knew she had for we gave her a diary the year she came out in London. We wanted her to be able to look back, read about her first Season. What a terrible memory that year ended up being for her."

Her aunt fumbled in her reticule and pulled out a handkerchief, dabbing at her eyes and nose. "She had been so happy, Molly. So full of promise and dreams. The day she died was a relief in the end, for her eyes had long stared at us as if in death. Her heart was broken and would never heal."

"And by your husband." Her uncle stood, helping his wife to stand. "You are welcome to search our London house for a diary if you think it'll help you ease your guilt."

Molly stood, ignoring the barb that embedded deep into her heart. She had hurt her family, and if what they had just stated was true, her husband had been Laura's lover. Despair washed over her, and she fought not to let the emotion make her panic. She walked her aunt and uncle to the front door.

"We are headed home today, we do not wish to stay in London a moment longer than necessary. Laura birthed her child in our London home. If the diary is to be found anywhere, it will be in that home. You are welcome to go there and search. We have a housekeeper, and two maids who live there, and you may ask them for entrance."

Molly nodded, handing her aunt her pelisse. "I am so very sorry to hurt you in this way. I fell in love, I did not know the truth of whom I fell in love with."

Her aunt reached out, clasping her cheek with her gloved hand. Molly reached up, holding her aunt's hand to her face. "We love you, our dearest Molly, and therefore we hope that you find a different answer to the one we've given you today, but when the truth does come out, and you feel you have nowhere to turn, please know you always have us. We shall never turn you away, no matter what you have done."

"Thank you," she said, a lump wedged in her throat. She stood at the door as they walked down the few steps to enter their carriage. Molly watched them go, thinking over what she would do. If Laura's diary held Hugh's name, her marriage would be over. Her future forever changed to the one she thought she would have when she'd said her vows. She closed the door, turning for the stairs, weary and in need of rest. Tomorrow she would face the answer she sought. Today had already been trying enough.

~

*H*ugh watched from the library door as Molly farewelled her aunt and uncle before returning upstairs to her room. He hated to see her so conflicted, sad, and lonely with the choice that she had to make. Desperate that he was, he'd spent the past hour listening in on her discussion with her family. The truth of his conduct was out there, he just needed to find it.

One glimmer of hope that had shone through was the mention of a diary. He could only hope that when Molly found the journal and God save him, he hoped she did, that he would be vindicated and proved innocent in this whole mess.

He knew he could not push her with her choice, make her believe him, he'd tried that enough already and had come up against a brick wall each time. She had to know the truth for them to have any chance of a future together.

Any chance of getting her down the aisle a second time to ensure their marriage was legitimate.

Hugh shut the door and walked over to the fire, leaning against the marble mantle. He glanced about the room, his brother's office, not that he'd been taking care of the estates very well since Hugh had lived in Rome. His brother had turned to gambling if the many IOUs in his desk drawer were any indication.

Within a few days of being back in London, Hugh had settled his brother's debts and paid off any accounts he had outstanding around town. Had his brother been trying to ruin the family? That he could never know, but it certainly seemed fiscally that way.

He slumped into a nearby chair and rested his head in his hands. If Laura's diary was never found, Hugh would have to set out to win Molly's trust and love. He could not live without her. To not see her smiling face at him every morning on the pillow next to him. Watch as her cheeks blossomed into a delightful, rosy hue whenever he said anything inappropriate. He couldn't live separately from the one person that was the sole reason his heart kept beating.

And soon they would have a child. A son or daughter that was part of both of them. He did not want to raise the child without her, nor did he wish to only see the child when Molly bade him access. To be a family meant he needed her here with him, sharing their lives and everything else that came their way.

His stomach roiled with the idea that she would come up empty-handed when she searched her aunt and uncle's home. If Laura had burned her diary before she passed, there was no one left to know the truth.

A chill ran down his spine at the possibility that they

could be severed from each other forever for a crime he had not committed. But would she trust him even if there was no one to tell her different to what she believed? If she loved him, she would trust his word, for God knows, he was not a liar. He would swear even on his own child's life, that it was not him who had ruined Miss Laura Cox, but his brother, St. Albans.

CHAPTER 16

*M*olly slumped back on her heels, staring at her cousin's bedroom, the bedding pulled off, scattered about the floor, and thoroughly searched. The few loose floorboards that she had found had been lifted, and with nothing to show for her efforts beneath them. She glanced down at her arm, blackened from the soot that had tarnished her clothing as she reached up and searched the chimney. With the assistance of a maid, Molly had moved furniture, emptied drawers, and padded the garments still occupying those cupboards, and nothing. Not a trace of this supposed diary.

It was not here, at least not in this room. Laura's chance to tell the truth, to declare once and for all who had wronged her, was not to be found. Perhaps she had burned it, for reasons only Laura herself could fathom. Molly did not blame her. To read the pages of a diary, one that would have initially been filled with love and adoration, of secrets and trysts would be a cause of despair if those moments of affection were no longer hers to have.

Molly would have burned her memories as well.

A little flutter caught her by surprise, and she reached for her stomach, her breath catching. She waited with bated breath to feel the movement again. She lent a half-laugh, half-sob when the little fluttering happened again.

Her baby. Their baby. The love of her life's child and the very man over whom she had to make a choice.

To trust and love him, or leave.

Molly pulled herself up and started for the door. She could not make a choice here, in her cousin's bedroom and where she passed. She needed to go to the one place she had always felt safe at home and at peace.

Within an hour, she was sitting in her best friend's drawing room, waiting for Evie to make an appearance. Her friend bustled into the room, her hair haphazardly pinned atop her head, as if she'd just risen from her bed.

Molly kissed her cheek, pushing down the pang of jealously of no longer having such afternoons abed with her husband. Of scurrying away to make love for as long as they wished. "I do apologize, Evie. I hope I have not imposed."

"Never, my darling." Evie rang for tea and sat across from her, taking in her rumpled gown and fixing the fishcu. "I was merely upstairs with Finn."

Heat bloomed on Evie's cheeks just as a footman knocked on the door, entering with the silver tea tray. Molly bit back her grin as she pulled off her gloves, setting them aside. "I do not know what to do, and I need your guidance."

"Anything, dearest."

"I saw my aunt and uncle, and they have confirmed what I imagined the worst. They do indeed believe the gentleman who seduced my cousin to her downfall was

Hugh. He, of course, is adamant that he was not to blame. I do not know whom to believe."

"Does knowing that perhaps Hugh made a mistake in his youth change the way you feel about him? I know what he is accused of is very bad, the *ton* talk of nothing but his downfall and flee from England, but that will be nothing if you love him."

Evie's face swam as the tears Molly had been so stoically holding at bay, burst free. She sniffed. "I love him still. So much that it hurts to think of not being with him, but Laura was my cousin. I was sent away to France because of my family's fear of future rogues taking advantage of me, as poor as I was."

"You are very beautiful, Molly. I can understand your family being worried after such an event."

"I want Hugh, but to love him, despite what he has done means I lose my family. It would mean that all I've ever thought about the situation, my ideals and morals are worthless because I have chosen the very man who created the whole mess." An impossible choice and one she did not wish to make. "I know that Laura was not innocent in all this, she chose to give herself to him, but he could have married her, instead of taking the easy way out and fleeing the country. Hugh could have shouted from the rooftops that his brother had wronged an innocent young woman and be damned the consequences."

Evie stared at her, her eyes full of pity and concern. "I think you just made your decision, my dear," she said, clasping her hand. "But before you do, remember that Hugh was young, a boy of twenty. To go up against one's family, his brother a duke no less, would indeed be very hard. He fled, but that may have been because there was little left for him to do. No other option given to him."

Molly stared at her friend for a long moment, thinking over her words. His choice had he been innocent of the crime would not have been easy, that was true. But if Hugh was the gentleman who had ruined Laura, there was no forgiving of that fact. She would be lying to herself, going against everything she ever believed if she forgave such a sin.

The lump in her throat burned, and as much as she tried to swallow past it, it would not shift. However, was she to leave the man she loved behind? Commence a life where it was only ever half-lived?

"Remember, we're always here for you, my dear."

Molly nodded. She would need her friends more than ever in the coming months. Oh, who was she fooling? Years to come.

~

*H*ugh looked up from his desk, the many letters to staff at St. Albans Abby before his brother's death scattered before him. He would chase down every last servant in England who worked here and the many estates he owned if it meant that he could find a single one of them who knew of his brother's liaison with Miss Cox. His life, his ability to keep his wife, depended on it. He could not fail her in this as well.

He'd failed her once before, he would not do it again.

Molly knocked on his door, waiting at the threshold before coming into the room. Hugh stood, striding over to her and pulling her inside. "You're very pale. What is wrong? Is the baby well?"

She didn't say a word, allowed him to place her onto

the settee in front of the fire before he went back and shut the door, giving them privacy.

"I was unable to find Laura's diary, as I had hoped. If she had it with her in London during the time of her child's birth, it is no longer there." She shrugged. "Perhaps it never was."

He sat beside her, the pit of his stomach in knots. Would Molly believe him, or continue to think ill of him? How could she not trust him to be telling the truth? The notion she did not know him well enough to believe him ate at the organ beating in his chest.

"Not finding this diary, what does that mean for us, Molly?" Her answer meant everything to him. If she chose to believe him, trust him, and love him, his life would be fulfilled. After his father had died, the love he'd once known as a child became obsolete. He needed his wife to love him, to understand what he was saying as fact, for it was.

"I'm sorry, Hugh. I cannot stay here."

Hugh stood, distancing himself from her. He needed a moment to think, to take in what she was saying. His stomach roiled at the thought of losing her, and for a moment, he thought he may cast up his accounts. "You do not believe me still. I did not do what you accuse me of, damn it, Molly. I hardly knew Laura, and that is the God's honest truth. If you choose to believe my lying mother, my bastard of a brother over me, then I suppose perhaps you should leave."

"What are you saying?" She looked up at him, her eyes filled with tears, and he wanted to go to her, beg her to change her mind. To not look at him with eyes that were a mirror image of his.

Heartbroken.

"You may have use of St. Albans Abby in Kent. I will visit prior to the child's birth and we will marry to ensure its legitimacy. I will be a good father to him or her, but I will not be staying in England forever. I want to return to Rome and expect my son or daughter to learn of his or her life there."

"I did not want this for us. You understand that, do you not?"

He dismissed her words, hurt, and disappointment riding hard on his heels. "What difference does it make now? You have made your choice, and you choose to believe gossip and falsehoods over the man you're supposed to love. I suppose the few weeks that we spent together in Rome meant more to me than they did you."

She stood, coming over to stand before him. "You cannot think that to be true. I loved and adored you."

A bark of laughter escaped at her words. She flinched at the sound. "Loved and adored. All past tense and precisely what our marriage has become. Past tense." He strode for the door, wrenching it open so forcefully that it slammed against the wall with a resounding thwack. "I shall order your belongings to be packed and loaded onto a carriage first thing tomorrow morning. Good day to you, Duchess."

Hugh beat a path toward the front door, ignoring the fact that his vision swam in unshed tears. How could she not judge him justly? Had someone accused her of such crimes, he certainly would have stood by her, not allowed anything to tarnish her name.

He blindly strode across Grosvenor Square, ignoring any who greeted him. He needed a drink. That's what he'd do. He'd go to Whites and get blind drunk, and maybe a night of gambling would soothe his hurt.

The notion was almost as absurd as the idea that Molly would change her mind. That he'd return home later this evening and find her warm in his bed. There was no future here. Not anymore. He had hoped that their life could be both in England and Italy, but it would seem that it was not to be.

For years he'd been known as the villainous younger brother of the Duke of St. Albans. Well, now they could keep him that way. The fight to clear his name fled, and his shoulders slumped. Let the *ton* and his wife believe what they wanted. They could all bloody well damn go to the devil.

CHAPTER 17

St. Albans Abby – Kent

The Season ended in town, and fall turned the leaves orange and brown across the land. Soon winter would be upon them, and so too would her time to have her child. Their child.

Molly had moved down to the ducal country estate in Kent after her inability to find the diary of her cousin and read in Laura's own words what had really happened that Season all those years ago.

The days stretched endlessly without Hugh, and Molly found herself thinking more and more about what her husband was doing why she was rusticating in the country. She read, of course, did needlepoint, walked about the estate, learning the lay of the lands, and the tenant farmers who worked for Hugh, but it was not the same.

She missed him.

Dreadfully so, and a little part of her mind would not let go of the hurt, the devastation she had read in his eyes the day she parted from him in London. An awful gnawing feeling kept her awake at night, telling her that she'd made a mistake. That it was his elder brother and not Hugh who had done her cousin wrong.

That she should have believed him above everyone else.

The more she spoke to the staff here at the Abby, the more she doubted what society and her family had come to accept. The late duke was not missed. In fact, he was tantamount to a bully if Hugh's sister, who returned last week from Bath, explained him to be.

Since her return, Sarah had been a godsend, keeping her company and helping her to know of the family dynamics that Hugh had grown up with. All of those things, including Hugh's adamant statement that he was innocent, culminated in her change of mind.

Which left another problem for her to face.

However, was she to stand before Hugh and ask for forgiveness? Ask him to forgive her for allowing what others believed to sway her opinion of him? She had left him. Her husband. The man she loved more than anyone or anything in this world, save for the child that grew in her womb.

He would never forgive her.

"Is that a carriage?"

Molly looked up from the Belle Assemble she was staring at and not the least interested in what lay in her lap and glanced toward the front drive. They were seated in the parlor that sat just off the entrance hall, the room giving its occupants full view of anyone who visited the estate.

The carriage was traveling faster than it ought, and Molly stood, going to the window to see who it was that had come. Sarah joined her, her brow furrowed as a woman all but bolted from the vehicle before it even stopped.

"I've never seen the lady before. Do you know her?" Sarah asked, turning toward her.

Molly was already moving toward the front foyer just as her aunt stepped into the room. Her attention immediately snapped to the cloth parcel she held in her hands, held closed by a frayed pink ribbon.

"Aunt, whatever are you doing here?" Molly kissed her cheek, hope blooming in her soul that her aunt's arrival could mean something in regards to Laura and her diary.

She was not wrong. "I found it. I found Laura's diary. Here," she said, handing it to her. "Read it."

Molly took the parcel. She pulled the ribbon, untying the knot, and glanced at what lay inside. Pages upon pages of letters, love notes, and in Laura's own hand, her own thoughts and dreams.

"I thought this lost forever. However, did you find it?"

Molly started toward the parlor, her mind scrambling to find a letter from the gentleman whom Laura had loved. The word Henry stood out like a blemish on a nose. Her eyes scanned the notes, the adulations, the longing, the sweet words between the two. Laura's sincere and Henry's, the late Duke of St. Albans a means and ways toward getting what he wanted. Laura in his bed.

"You could have kept this from me. To show me this does not put Laura into the best light, along with the duke. Even so, I cannot tell you how very happy I am to see these letters."

Sarah sat beside Molly, reaching out to clasp her about the shoulders. "I told you Hugh was innocent. Henry was a cad, a troublesome boy who grew up to be a selfish, arrogant man. I like to think that Hugh and I are like our father, kind, honest, and honorable. Henry took after Mama in all his wayward traits."

Molly's aunt studied Sarah a moment as if only just noticing her presence. "Aunt Jossalin, this is Lady Sarah Farley, Hugh's younger sister. Sarah, this is my aunt Jossalin Cox, Laura's mama."

Sarah inclined her head a little. "I am happy to meet you, Mrs. Cox, and I'm sorry for all that you've suffered at my family's hand."

"It was not your doing, my dear." Her aunt's lips lifted into a semblance of a smile, but pain lurked in her blue orbs—pain left by the late duke's treatment of her daughter and what ultimately happened to Molly's cousin.

"Where did you find it?" Molly asked, skimming through pages and pages of notes. Henry was certainly a gentleman who knew how to play to a woman's heart-strings. The sweet gestures, his appreciation of her gowns at balls, and how her cousin comported herself within society would make anyone think that an offer of marriage would be forthcoming.

"A maid had packed it away with some of Laura's things upon her passing. The trunk was forgotten in the attic. On a whim, I decided to look through her old things, reminisce I suppose. See if I could still smell her." Tears welled in her aunt's eyes, and she dabbed at her face with her hand. "It was sitting atop of all her gowns and shawls. I was so lost in my grief when we were in London. I did not think of her things that were left to pack away at our country house. The staff took the initiative and did that for us, and I never sought to check on that myself. I wish I had, for had I done so, these many weeks you've been living estranged from His Grace would not have happened."

Molly reached out, clasping her aunt's hand. "What I do not understand is why Laura did not name her lover. The man who ruined her. Why protect the late duke when he'd treated her so poorly?"

"This letter may explain that, my dear." Her aunt handed her a missive that she carried on her person.

Molly unfolded the note, discolored by time. She gasped, unable to accept what she was reading. "He promised her that although he could not marry her, he would take care of her after the birth of their child. Send her away to one of his country estates and gift her a house on his land, including a maid and cook. Do you think he would have done this, Aunt?"

"I do not know, but if you read farther, he states that should she tell anyone of their affair, name him as the father of her child and not Hugh, he would leave her to rot."

"Sounds like Henry," Sarah said, her mouth pinched in a displeased line.

Molly looked back at her aunt. "So how did it come about that Hugh was cited as the villain?"

"That, my dear, is your uncle's cross to bear. We knew someone had meddled with our Laura. After all, she was pregnant, terribly discouraged and lonely, leading up to the birth of her son. We had not been blind in society, we had seen Laura about the St. Albans brothers, but then one evening, your uncle remembered seeing the then Lord Hugh Farley talking to Laura, and he believed what the duchess was saying.

"By the time this occurred, Lord Farley was already bundled into a carriage and headed for the continent. Spain supposedly, but that was what society was tittering. They refused to help Laura, the duchess would not allow either of her sons to marry a woman whose inheritance came from trade. That was not good enough for the St. Albans."

Molly placed the missive in with the rest of the letters and closed the parcel, placing it on the small table before them. "I know what that conversation had been about. Hugh told me himself. He told Laura to keep away from Henry. Tried to warn her of his brother's fickleness, his using nature when it came to women. I'm ashamed I did not believe Hugh any more than Laura had."

"You can, however, my dear, repair the damage the late duke and his mother have caused. You can mend the rift between you and His Grace. My Laura did not have the chance to fix her mistake, but you do. I suggest you return to town post-haste."

"You're right," Molly said, standing and striding toward the door. She wrenched it open, yelling for Thomas the butler.

The butler appeared from somewhere behind the stairs, bowing. "Your Grace?"

"I'll be leaving today for London. Have my maid pack my things and prepare a carriage. We need to leave within the hour."

The old household retainer started at her demand, before bowing and moving off to do her bidding. She turned, facing her aunt and sister-in-law. "Thank you, Aunt Jossalin for bringing me this news. I know it could not have been easy."

"Laura loved you like a sister, and would not want you to suffer because of her love for the duke's brother. Had she been of the right mind and known that your husband had been deemed the gentleman responsible for her downfall, she would not have allowed that."

"Go and change, Molly. You have a husband to claim and make yours. I shall see you soon when you return to Kent."

Molly nodded, her stomach knotted in nerves. What would Hugh say to her when she confronted him? Would he forgive her for thinking the worst? For not trusting and believing him, the man she loved above all others.

She ran up the stairs, determination riding hard on her heels. She would not let him push her aside. Not allow this mistake made by others to sever the love they had. That she still had for him.

If it were the last thing she did on this earth, she would win him back. There was no alternative to be had and no time to waste.

CHAPTER 18

*H*ugh tried to not feel sorry for himself or lose himself in the decanter of whiskey that he'd almost downed since the previous day. He lay in his bed, staring up at the ceiling. His eyes refused to focus on the mural, and so what he knew to be women floating in clouds, their roman togas and long flowing hair about their shoulders was nothing but a blur. Shadows that were oddly familiar to his life at present.

However had he allowed her to leave? Whyever had he done so? He'd done nothing wrong. He should have demanded she believe him. Told her as her husband that she would stand by his side or, or…

He sighed, groaning as the room spun. Who was he fooling? He could no more control his wife than he could control the ocean.

The sound of quickened footsteps echoed in the hall outside his room, and he sat up, leaning on his arms. Who was that running through the house in the middle of the night?

His bedroom door flew open, and his mouth dried at

the sight of his wife, hair askew, her afternoon gown rumpled from a day and well into the evening travel. She ripped off her gloves and dropped them at her feet, reaching behind her and shutting the door with a decided bang.

His speech seemed to have evaded his ability. His body tightened as it always did when Molly was about. He tensed, longed, and ached to hear her voice, to feel her touch.

When had he fallen so very hard for his wife?

A small smile lifted his lips, knowing the answer to that question. The moment she had seen Rome from his upstairs balcony the first time. The memory of it now sent a pang of longing to ripple through him so hard he had to force himself to breathe. Her long, silken locks flowing over her finely boned shoulders, her mouth open in awe of the city beneath her. He'd fought the urge to kiss her plump lips then and there and should have known she would mean change was coming to his life.

A change well overdue and most welcome.

"Hugh." His name was a rushed whisper as if she were relieved to find him here. He devoured the sight of her, the rounded belly of his child that grew in her womb. Her long legs and heaving breasts from her sprint upstairs. Hell, he'd missed her. He should have dragged her back to London and told everyone to go to the devil with their rumor-mongering. He loved his wife, and she ought to be with him.

And now she was here. But why?

"What are you doing in London?" The question came out as a croak, and he cleared his throat, watching as she took the steps that separated them, coming to stand beside the bed. Unable to help himself, he sat up, twisting to perch at the edge of the bed. She was so close, under an arm's touch from him. Hugh reached out and cradled her stomach, hating that he'd missed even a month of being with her.

She stared down at him, her eyes round with concern. Her hands shook at her sides, and he clasped them in his. "Tell me, my love?"

Molly slumped at his words, sitting beside him and pulling him into an embrace. She held him tight as if she never wished to let him go. He would never allow her to go anywhere from him again, that was for certain, if she let him.

"I was wrong. I judged you unfairly, and I'm so sorry, Hugh. My aunt found Laura's diary, and as you said, Henry was her lover, the father of her child."

This was no news to Hugh. Of course Henry was the father, proving that point was difficult, however, when there was no proof and his family had lied to persuade others that he was guilty of the crime. "Of course, he was, my love, but I am glad that you're finally on my side on the matter."

She pulled back, her lashes wet with tears, and his heart lurched in his chest. He wiped her cheeks, hating to see her upset. "I do not blame you, Molly. No one believes me, nor will they unless your cousin's diary is published, and I would never do that to your family."

"However will we clear your name in the eyes of society? They need to know the truth. Blame your brother, not you. It is unfair for them to treat you as they will, as I have. I'm so sorry, Hugh. I understand if you can never forgive me. I cannot forgive myself."

He pushed her wayward locks from her face, needing to see her clearly. "I was angry and upset, but I could also understand, my love. Laura was your cousin, and you thought her tarnished by my hand. Without proof, even I would struggle to believe you should you have been the villain."

She sniffed, meeting his gaze. "No, you would not. You said yourself that you would believe me before anyone else, and I did not offer you the same trust."

He shrugged, knowing it would be harder for a woman to believe a man than a man to believe a woman. "It does not matter now, my love. That you're here is all I want."

"I love you, Hugh. I should have believed you and no one else. I'm sorry that I did not come sooner. Not until I knew the truth."

He frowned, reaching behind her and playing with the ties of her dress. "Were you thinking of coming back to me? Before you knew the truth?"

She nodded, her hands untying his cravat. "I was. I missed you so very much. Even with the company of your sister, I was lonely. What you were accused of, I could not get out of my mind, and the more I thought upon it, the more I realized it was not true. That I trusted you enough to believe your word over that of others. People that I did not even know. I had all but decided to return to town when my aunt arrived."

He would kiss Molly's aunt the next time he saw the woman. Thank her profusely that she'd continued her search for the elusive diary. "Whether you came to your decision on your own merit or because of your aunt's visit, know that I'm happy that you're here. I've missed you so much."

Hugh could wait no longer, and he kissed her, clasped her cheeks, and drank deep from her lips. Her mouth opened, their tongues melding. His heart beat hard in his chest, a resounding drum he was sure she could hear.

"You taste of spirits." Molly pulled his shirt free from his breeches before ripping it off over his head, throwing it aside. "You're not a little foxed by any chance, are you, Your Grace?"

"I'm drunk with happiness." He grinned, groaning as her hand slipped against his falls, and she popped his buttons free. Hugh closed his eyes, sucking in a breath as her touch clasped his cock, stroking him with an expertise that left him aching.

"I've missed you so much. All of you." She kissed him, pushing him to lie back on his bed before straddling his hips.

"Your clothes. Remove them."

She shuffled off his lap, and he took the opportunity to move farther onto the bed. He lay back, his arms behind his head, watching her through hooded eyes as she slipped the gown off her shoulders to pool at her slippered feet. Her shift was all but translucent, and his cock hardened further at the sight of her. In the moonlight, her eyes blazed with need, and he took a calming breath, wanting to pleasure her before seeking his own release.

With a wicked smirk, she slowly untied the laces at the front of her shift. The material gaped, giving him a delightful view of her ample breasts. She pushed the shift off her shoulders, and it too landed with a swoosh on the floor.

She kneeled on the bed, crawling over to straddle his groin. "I want you so much." The siren that his wife was turning into... She slid against his cock, her heat, the wetness that coated him told him she needed him as much as he wanted her.

So deliciously hot. He wanted to roll her over, fuck her until he no longer knew where he started and she ended, but he could not. After the child was born, there would be plenty of time for that. Tonight would be different. He'd allow her to take him, use him to find release and then, and only then, would he come.

Hugh reached up, circling her breasts with his hands. She sighed, her nipples pebbling into tight knots. He sat up, pulling her against him and covered one nipple with his mouth. He flicked the beaded flesh with his tongue, giving it a love bite or two before soothing it yet again with his mouth.

Her breathing ragged, she reached between them, taking him in hand. His cock twitched at the feel of her hot, welcoming core. She lowered herself onto him, wrapping her arms about his neck as she embedded herself fully.

"Oh, yes," she sighed.

The urge to take her and make her his again rode hard within him, but he breathed deep, let his beautiful wife set her own pace, and find her pleasure and release. He held her tight against him, helping her undulate upon him. She was such a perfect fit, breathy moans, and sighs all the stimulation he needed to remain patient and wait.

His turn would come.

*M*olly pushed Hugh back onto the bedding, holding his shoulders as she rocked up and down on his cock. So hard and fulfilling. Teasing that special little place within her that craved and mourned the loss of him all these weeks.

Her body did not feel like her own. Everything was

more sensitive, her breasts, her cunny, everything ached and wept more than before. It only added to the pleasure, to the need that rode hard within her.

She took all of him, rocked against him until the pleasure, the sensations thrumming through her veins were too much. A pulsing started at her core, exploding throughout her body. Molly moaned his name, took him until her body no longer convulsed around his manhood.

"Make me come," he demanded, not forcing anything upon her, willing to be at her mercy.

His command was like an elixir, and she continued, riding him with vigor. His manhood swelled inside her. His fingers dug into her hips, slamming her down upon him before he gasped, moaned her name, and spent himself long and sure inside her.

She kissed his words from his lips, taking his mouth in a searing kiss before slumping at his side, her leg carelessly laying over his waist.

He shifted, reaching down to pull the bedding over them both, before pulling her into the crook of his arm. His lips brushed her temple, his hand idly running along her spine.

"Does this mean you'll be staying here in London or at least staying with me?"

She looked up at him, and their eyes met. Her heart thumped hard in her chest over what she felt for this man. A man she'd allowed what others believed in him to cloud her own thoughts and beliefs. Never again would she doubt him, not for anyone.

"Can we return to St. Albans Abby in Kent? The Season is over, and I want to prepare for the baby. Make your childhood home, our home, our child's home."

He kissed her again, seemingly unable to get enough of

her. Not that she minded, she loved being in his arms. This, right now, was what felt true. To be here again with her husband, her lover, and friend was all she needed.

"On one condition," he said, pulling back.

She glanced at him, wondering what he meant. "I will do anything. I hope you know that now."

His wicked grin sent her blood to pump. "We shall leave in the morning, but only if you marry me."

Tears blurred her vision, but she nodded. "Yes, of course I will marry you. Again."

He kissed her with such tenderness that she knew her heart would never beat for anyone else. After a time, she snuggled into his side, allowed the constant drum of his heartbeat to lull her to sleep. She had missed this, just the two of them, alone together. She pulled him tighter into her hold, silently promising to love him always.

And forever.

EPILOGUE

Early December 1829- St Albans Abby, Kent

Their baby boy, Lord Oliver Hugh Farley, Marquess Brentwood, future Duke of St. Albans lay snuggled in Hugh's arms, both father and son asleep before the roaring fire in the duke's study at the Abby. The room had become a sanctuary for the family. Lady Sarah, also retired here most evenings as the house was in an uproar with the forthcoming Christmas House party they were hosting.

Molly sat before the fire on the floor, going over all the acceptances they had received. So many people seemed only too pleased to believe the new Duke of St. Albans of his innocence in his brother's dealing with Miss Cox. With the help of the Duke of Whitstone, other friends, and that of her aunt who had made an appearance at a London ball, had gifted Hugh his absolution of doing anything wrong. Had placed the blame solely on who it was who had done the unforgivable damage, Henry, his brother.

"There are so many people coming. You have twenty

acceptances here alone. Are there many more who will be in attendance?" Sarah asked, sitting on the settee and staring down at the letters scattered about the floor.

"No, this is all of them now. I did not think that so many people would agree to attend. It is winter, after all. Terribly cold time to travel." Molly chuckled, marking off the names on her list. "I suppose it is only fortunate that your home is so very large. We shall at least be able to give everyone a room to themselves."

"Our home," Hugh said, meeting her gaze, his eyes heavy with sleep.

She sighed, adoring him more and more with every passing day they were here. "Our home," she corrected herself. She turned back to Sarah, raising her brow. "You did not want anyone to attend? It is not too late to invite someone if you wish."

"No, there is no one I would suggest. As far as I'm concerned, society can go hang after what they did to Hugh for all those years. In turn, made me have to live here in England with Mama and Henry. It was not to be borne."

Hugh chuckled, the baby fussing in his arms at the sound of his words. "Had I known it was so very bad for you here, Sarah, I would have come home and taken you back to Rome with me."

She shrugged, giving her brother a small smile. "I do not blame you, Hugh, but I am holding you to your promise to take me to Italy after winter. I'm so in need of an adventure. I want to see where you have made your second home and see Rome and its history."

"It is a marvelous place that will forever hold a special place in my heart." Molly glanced at Hugh, the love burning hot in his eyes stealing her breath.

"And I, my love." Their son started to cry, and Hugh's soothing voice calmed him. He lay him over his shoulder, patting his back, and within a moment, the baby was settled once again.

"How many weeks are we to endure these guests?"

Molly chuckled at Sarah's question. "Only four, which is not too many, I think. And you will love my friends, Sarah, just as much as they will love you."

"I'm sure I will, and they will be the only ones, but mark my words that if anyone should even mumble anything about Hugh and the scandal that followed him about for all those years, I shall not be held responsible for my outburst. Nor will I take well to having a set down from my brother concerning my sticking up for you either."

Hugh nodded, kissing their son on his little bald head. "I promise not to chastise you should you say something in my defense."

"You needn't worry about that, however." Molly stood, placing the replies on Hugh's desk before coming back and sitting next to her husband. "I did not invite anyone whom we're not on close terms with. Everyone coming will be jolly and happy to be here to celebrate the Christmas period, and Hugh's return to England after all these years."

Sarah sighed, smiling at them both. "I am happy for you, Hugh and Molly. You deserve happiness after all that you endured. I promise to be on my best behavior."

Molly smiled. Hugh chuckled, a disbelieving tone to his laugh. "I shall believe that when I see it, sister dear. If what I remember of you and your antics, you were always a little rascal."

Sarah raised her chin in defiance. "I have never been a rascal, merely a woman of independent thought. Like your wife."

Molly met Hugh's eyes, reveling in the love that she saw staring back at her. "If that is the case, then, my dear sister, just as I've said to my beautiful, smart, and kind wife, please do not ever change."

Had she been standing, her legs would have wobbled at the sweet declaration. She closed the small space between them and kissed him, oblivious of their company. "I love you too," she whispered for only him to hear, her heart full and incandescently happy.

The sound of Sarah mumbling about kissing before her faded as she left the room. Molly chuckled, reaching up to play with the little fluff of hair on their son's head.

"Happy?" Hugh asked her, meeting her eyes.

She swallowed the lump in her throat, unable to voice just how much she was. "Very much so."

His wicked grin made her stomach somersault. "Me too."

They smiled at each other a moment before she laid her head on his spare shoulder, watching their boy. Their little family. A piece of paradise not in Rome, but snowy, country Kent.

It warmed her heart as hot as the Mediterranean sun had her life.

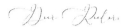

Dear Reader,

Thank you for taking the time to read *Kiss Me, Duke*! I hope you enjoyed the fifth book in my League of Unweddable Gentlemen series. If you're like me, you love traveling, and so I hope you enjoyed the small taste of Rome that was in this book. It goes without saying that it's one of the most fascinating cities in the world.

I adore my readers, and I'm so thankful for your support with my books. If you're able, I would appreciate an honest review of *Kiss Me, Duke*. As they say, feed an author, leave a review!

If you think this is the last book in this series, don't despair. Soon to be released in a Christmas box set is, Lady Sarah Farley's story. More details on this to come, so stay tuned.

Tamara Gill

ONLY AN EARL WILL DO

TO MARRY A ROGUE, BOOK 1

The reigning queen of London society, Lady Elizabeth Worthingham, has her future set out for her. Marry well, and marry without love. An easy promise to make and one she owed her family after her near ruinous past that threatened them all. And the rakish scoundrel Henry Andrews, Earl of Muir who's inability to act a gentleman when she needed one most would one day pay for his treachery.

. . .

Returning to England after three years abroad, Henry is determined to make the only woman who captured his heart his wife. But the icy reception he receives from Elizabeth is colder than his home in the Scottish highlands. As past hurts surface and deception runs as thick as blood, so too does a love that will overcome all obstacles, unless a nameless foe, determined with his own path, gets his way and their love never sees the light of day...

CHAPTER 1

England 1805 – Surrey

"*Y*ou're ruined."

Elizabeth stood motionless as her mother, the Duchess of Penworth, paced before the lit hearth, her golden silk gown billowing out behind her, the deep frown between her eyes daring anyone to follow her. "No. Let me rephrase that. The family is ruined. All my girls, their futures, have been kicked to the curb like some poor street urchins."

Elizabeth, the eldest of all the girls, swiped a lone tear from her cheek and fought not to cast up her accounts. "But surely Henry has written of his return." She turned to her father. "Papa, what did his missive say?" The severe frown lines between her father's brows were deeper than she'd ever seen them before, and dread pooled in her belly. What had she done? What had Henry said?

"I shall not read it to you, Elizabeth, for I fear it'll only upset you more, and being in the delicate condition you are we must keep you well. But never again will I allow the

Earl of Muir to step one foot into my home. To think," her father said, kicking at a log beside the fire, "that I supported him to seek out his uncle in America. I'm utterly ashamed of myself."

"No," Elizabeth said, catching her father's gaze. "You have nothing to be ashamed of. I do. I'm the one who lay with a man who wasn't my husband. I'm the one who now carries his child." The tears she'd fought so hard to hold at bay started to run in earnest. "Henry and I were friends, well, I thought we were friends. I assumed he'd do the right thing by our family, by me. Why is it that he'll not return?"

Her mother, quietly staring out the window, turned at her question. "Because his uncle has said no nephew of his would marry a strumpet who gave away the prize before the contracts were signed, and Henry apparently was in agreement with this statement."

Her father sighed. "There is an old rivalry between Henry's uncle and me. We were never friends, even though I noted Henry's father high in my esteem, as close as a brother, in fact. Yet his sibling was temperamental, a jealous cur."

"Why were you not friends with Henry's uncle, Papa?" He did not reply. "Please tell me. I deserve to know."

"Because he wished to marry your mama, and I won her hand instead. He was blind with rage, and it seems even after twenty years he wishes to seek revenge upon me by ruining you."

Elizabeth flopped onto a settee, shocked by such news. "Did Henry know of this between you and his uncle? Did you ever tell him?"

"No. I thought it long forgotten."

Elizabeth swallowed as the room started to swirl. "So, Henry has found his wealthy uncle and has been poisoned by his lies. The man has made me out to be a light-skirts of little character." She took a calming breath. "Tell me, does the letter really declare this to be Henry's opinion as well?"

The duke came and sat beside her. "It is of both their opinions, yes." He took her hand and squeezed it. "You need to marry, Elizabeth, and quickly. There is no other choice."

She stood, reeling away from her father and such an idea. To marry a stranger was worse than no marriage at all and falling from grace. "I cannot do that. I haven't even had a season. I know no one."

"A good friend of mine, Viscount Newland, recently passed. His son, Marcus, who is a little simple of mind after a fall from a horse as a child, is in need of a wife. But because of his ailment, no one will have him. They are desperate to keep the estate within the family and are looking to marry him off. It would be a good match for you both. I know it is not what you wanted, but it will save you and your sisters from ruin."

Elizabeth stood looking down at her father, her mouth agape with shock and not a little amount of disgrace. "You want me to marry a simpleton?"

"His speech is a little delayed only, otherwise he's a kind young man. I grant you he's not as handsome as Henry, but...well, we must do what's best in these situations."

Her mother sighed. "Lord Riddledale has called and asked for your hand once more. You could always accept his suit."

"Please, I would rather cut off my own hand than marry his lordship." Just the thought was enough to make her skin crawl.

"Well then, you will marry Lord Newland. I'm sorry,

but it must and will be done," her mother said, her tone hard.

Elizabeth walked to the window that looked toward the lake where she'd given herself to Henry. His sweet whispered words of love, of wanting her to wait for him, that as soon as he procured enough funds to support his Scottish estate they would marry, flittered through her mind. What a liar he'd turned out to be. All he wanted was her innocence and nothing else.

Anger thrummed through her and she grit her teeth. How dare Henry trick her in such a way? Made her fall in love with him, promised to be faithful and marry her when he returned. He never wished to marry her. Had he wanted to right now he would be on his way back to England.

She turned, staring at her parents who looked resigned to a fate none of them imagined possible or ever wanted. "I will marry Viscount Newland. Write them and organize the nuptials to take place within the month or sooner if possible. The child I carry needs a father and the viscount needs a wife."

"Then it is done." Her father stood, walking over to her and taking her hand. "Did Henry promise you anything, Elizabeth? The letter is so out of character for him, I've wondered since receiving it that it isn't really of his opinion but his uncle's only."

"He wanted me to wait for him, to give him time to save his family's estate. He did not wish to marry a woman for her money; he wanted to be a self-made man, I suppose."

"Lies, Elizabeth. All lies," her mother stated, her voice cold. "Henry has used you, I fear, and I highly doubt he'll ever come back to England or Scotland, for that matter."

Elizabeth swallowed the lump in her throat, not wanting to believe the man she'd given her heart to would treat her in such a way. She'd thought Henry was different, was a gentleman who loved her. At the look of pity her father bestowed on her, she pushed him aside and ran from the room.

She needed air, fresh, cooling, calming air. Opening the front door, the chilling icy wind hit her face, and clarity assailed. She'd go for a ride. Her mount Argo always made her feel better.

It took the stable hand only minutes to saddle her mount, and she was soon trotting away from the house, the only sound that of the snow crunching beneath her horse's hooves. The chill pierced through her gown, and she regretted not changing into a suitable habit, but riding astride in whatever they had on at the time was a normal practice for the children of the Duke of Penworth. Too much freedom as a child, all of them allowed to do whatever they pleased, and now that freedom had led her straight into the worst type of trouble.

She pushed her horse into a slow canter, her mind a kaleidoscope of turmoil. Henry, once her father's ward, a person she'd thought to call a friend, had betrayed her when she needed him most. Guilt and shame swamped her just as snow started to fall, and covered everything in a crystal white hue.

She would never forgive Henry for this. Yes, they'd made a mistake, a terrible lack of decorum on her behalf that she'd never had time to think through. But should the worst happen, a child, she had consoled herself that Henry would do right by her, return home and marry her.

How could she have been so wrong?

She clutched her stomach, still no signs that a little

child grew inside, and as much as she was ruined, could possibly ruin her family, she didn't regret her condition, and nor would she birth this child out of wedlock. Lord Newland would marry her since his situation was not looked upon favorably by the ton; it was a match that would suit them both.

Guilt pricked her soul that she would pass off Henry's child as Lord Newland's, but what choice did she have? Henry would not marry her, declare the child his. Elizabeth had little choice. There was nothing else to be done about it.

A deer shot out of the bracken, and Argo shied, jumping sharply to the side. Elizabeth screamed as her seat slipped. The action unbalanced her and she fell, hitting the ground hard.

Luckily, the soft snow buffered her fall, and she sat up, feeling the same as she had when upon her horse. She rubbed her stomach, tears pooling in her eyes with the thought that had she fallen harder, all her problems would be over. What a terrible person she was to think such a thing, and how she hated Henry that his refusal of her had brought such horrendous thoughts to mind.

Argo nuzzled her side as she stood; reaching for the stirrup, she hoisted herself back onto her mount. Wiping the tears from her eyes, Elizabeth promised no more would be shed over a boy, for that was surely what Henry still was, an immature youth who gave no thought to others.

She would marry Viscount Newland, try and make him happy as much as possible when two strangers came together in such a union, and be damned anyone who mentioned the name Henry Andrews, Lord Muir to her again.

◇

America 1805 – New York Harbor

*H*enry raised his face to the wind and rain as the packet ship sailed up the Hudson River. The damp winter air matched the cold he felt inside, numbing the pain that hadn't left his core since farewelling the shores of England. And now he was here. America. The smoky city just waking to a new day looked close enough to reach out and touch, and yet his true love, Elizabeth, was farther away than she'd ever been before.

He rubbed his chest and huddled into his greatcoat. The five weeks across the ocean had dragged, endless days with his mind occupied with only one thought: his Elizabeth lass.

He shut his eyes, bringing the vision of her to his mind, her honest, laughing gaze, the beautiful smile that had always managed to make his breath catch. He frowned, missing her as much as the highland night sky would miss the stars.

"So, Henry, lad, what's your plan on these great lands?" Henry took in the captain on the British Government packet; his graying whiskers across his jaw and crinkled skin about his eyes told of a man who'd lived at sea his entire life, and enjoyed every moment of it. He grinned. "Make me fortune. Mend a broken family tie if I can."

The captain lit a cheroot and puffed, the smoke soon lost in the misty air. "Ah, grand plans then. Any ideas on how you'll be making your fortune? I could use some tips myself."

"My uncle lives here. Owns a shipping company apparently, although I've yet to meet the man or see for myself if this is true. I'm hoping since he's done so well for himself he can steer me along the road to me own fortune."

The captain nodded, staring toward the bow. "It seems you have it all covered."

Henry started when the captain yelled orders for half-mast. He hoped the old man was right with his statement. The less time he stayed here the better it would be. He pushed away the thought that Elizabeth was due to come out in the forthcoming months, to be paraded around the ton like a delicious morsel of sweet meats. To be the center of attention, a duke's daughter ripe for the picking. He ground his teeth.

"I wish you good luck, Henry."

"Thank ye." The captain moved away, and he turned back to look at the city so unlike London or his highland home. Foreign and wrong on so many levels. The muddy waters were the only similarity to London, he mused, smiling a little.

Henry walked to the bow, leaning over the wooden rail. He sighed, trying to expel the sullen mood that had swamped him the closer they came to America. What he was doing here was a good thing, an honorable thing, something that if he didn't do, Elizabeth would be lost to him forever.

He couldn't have hated his grandfather more at that moment for having lost their fortune at the turn of a card all those years ago. It was a miracle his father had been able to keep Avonmore afloat and himself out of debtor's prison.

The crewmen preparing the packet ship for docking sounded around him, and he started toward the small room he'd been afforded for the duration of the trip. It was better than nothing; even if he'd not been able to stand up fully within the space, at least it was private and comfortable.

Determination to succeed, to ensure his and Elizabeth's future was secure, to return home as soon as he may, sparked within him. He would not fail; for once, the Earl of Muir would not gamble the estate's future away, but fight for its survival, earn it respectably just as his ancestors had.

And he would return home, marry his English lass, and spoil her for the remainder of their days. In Scotland.

Want to read more? Purchase, Only an Earl Will Do today!

LORDS OF LONDON SERIES
AVAILABLE NOW!

Dive into these charming historical romances! In this six-book series, Darcy seduces a virginal duke, Cecilia's world collides with a roguish marquess, Katherine strikes a deal with an unlucky earl and Lizzy sets out to conquer a very wicked Viscount. These stories plus more adventures in the Lords of London series! Available now through Amazon or read free with KindleUnlimited.

Lords of London

KISS THE WALLFLOWER SERIES
AVAILABLE NOW!

If the roguish Lords of London are not for you and wall-flowers are more your cup of tea, this is the series for you. My Kiss the Wallflower series, are linked through friendship and family in this four-book series. You can grab a copy on Amazon or read free through KindleUnlimited.

KISS THE WALLFLOWER - BOOKS 1-3 BUNDLE

KISS THE WALLFLOWER - BOOKS 4-6 BUNDLE

Lords of London Series

TO BEDEVIL A DUKE

TO MADDEN A MARQUESS

TO TEMPT AN EARL

TO VEX A VISCOUNT

TO DARE A DUCHESS

TO MARRY A MARCHIONESS

LORDS OF LONDON - BOOKS 1-3 BUNDLE

LORDS OF LONDON - BOOKS 4-6 BUNDLE

To Marry a Rogue Series

ONLY AN EARL WILL DO

ONLY A DUKE WILL DO

ONLY A VISCOUNT WILL DO

ONLY A MARQUESS WILL DO

ONLY A LADY WILL DO

TO MARRY A ROGUE - BOOKS 1-5 BUNDLE

A Time Traveler's Highland Love Series

TO CONQUER A SCOT

TO SAVE A SAVAGE SCOT

TO WIN A HIGHLAND SCOT

HIGHLAND LOVE - BOOKS 1-3 BUNDLE

A Stolen Season Series